# THE SHADOW ENCLAVE

## MITCH HERRON 2

### STEVE P. VINCENT

# 1

MITCH HERRON'S eyes flickered open for only a second before he squeezed them shut again. The fluorescent lighting was too harsh. It hurt.

His mind sifted multiple sensory inputs – the lighting, the gentle hum of machinery, the smell of disinfectant, the scratch of poor-quality bed sheets and the coppery taste of sleep – but none of it made sense.

It made no sense that he was still alive.

He lay on his back, drifting in and out of sleep, his body too weak to move. Time passed, but without a reference point he could've been there for minutes or hours or days or months. Any attempt to move exhausted him and when he tried to speak he produced an indecipherable mumble.

Nobody came to help him. He was adrift in an endless purgatory.

"Mitch! Wake up!"

It took Herron a second to process the voice whispering near his ear. He cracked his eyes open again, but it was like anvils were weighing down the lids and he drifted gently back to sleep.

"Mitch!" The female voice had been tentative before. Now it was urgent. "You need to wake up!"

Herron mumbled and opened his eyes again. This time he managed to keep them open long enough to see a woman in a white lab coat, inches away from him. Concern was etched on her face... he knew her. She'd been there at the end, when he'd died.

Should've died?

It took all of his effort to focus. He coughed out a word. "Erica."

A smile flashed across her face, quickly replaced by a frown. "We need to go."

"Go?" Herron's mind was still catching up. He was so tired. "Where?"

"Anywhere but here."

Herron blinked away the sleep. He didn't understand why she was so insistent on moving him, but he trusted her. "Okay."

She disconnected the IV lines from his arm, pulled the electrodes from his chest and removed the bed sheets covering his body. As she did, Herron tried to figure out what had happened to him. He remembered being in a lab, infected with a killer virus, giving Kearns the last remaining dose of the cure... but everything after that was a blank.

"Where...?"

"Not now." Kearns shushed him, gripped his hand tightly and helped him to sit up.

"Ugh." He already felt like the living dead, but it got worse. Nausea overwhelmed him like a punch to the stomach and he sagged back.

Kearns stopped him from toppling over by pulling on his arm and then putting hers behind his back. She whispered. "Mitch, I really need you to stand. They're coming."

Herron closed his eyes, took a deep breath and then opened them again. The nausea had subsided a little, so he swung his legs out of bed and put his feet on the floor. After another deep breath he stood. His legs gave out immediately and Kearns didn't have the strength to keep him upright. He landed hard on the floor, grunting as his head struck the bed frame on the way down.

A sharp pain lanced through his skull and coughing wracked his body. He pushed himself up, tasting metal in his mouth. He spat on the tiled floor and there was blood in his saliva. Kearns was urging him to stand, so he gripped the edge of the bed and climbed to his feet, his body aching like he'd just finished a marathon. He wanted desperately to rest, but one glance at Kearns told him there was no time to waste.

Whether from illness or sedation or both, Herron's legs were too weak to carry him for long and he was reluctant to put too much weight on Kearns, but there was no other way. He was a foot taller than the doctor, so he had to drape his arm over her shoulder while she wrapped one around his waist.

One of the deadliest assassins on Earth, relying on a 130-pound woman to help him walk.

Using her as a crutch, he stumbled in a strange lockstep toward the door. As they shuffled closer, Herron took the time to look around. The room had no features that'd identify where he was, except that he'd been in a regular hospital bed, surrounded by expensive equipment.

He frowned. "Where are we, Erica?"

"The CDC." She glanced at him and then back to the door. "I was able to stabilize you long enough to get you here. They produced more vaccine from my blood. We cured the virus... Look, I'll fill you in later. The cops are coming for you. Now you're better, the CDC has agreed to turn you over to them. They'll be on their way up."

He shook his head, trying to get his thoughts in order. Gradually it came back to him – how they'd wanted him on suspicion of kidnapping and how the trail of bodies he'd left across the country eradicating a band of bio terrorists would make that charge look like jaywalking.

Kearns pressed on his back and he allowed her to

move him forward, acting on instinct and trust because he had no other information and no other option. At the door, Kearns reached out for the handle... and stopped. Her eyes were filled with doubt as they probed his and it became clear to Herron how much she was risking here.

"I'm good." He forced a smile. Making it this far had consumed almost all of his energy and he had no idea how much further he had to go. But he'd make it. He had to.

\* \* \*

Herron pressed himself hard against the wall, his arm across Kearns' chest, holding her back. As the sound of footfalls gradually receded then disappeared entirely, he relaxed a little and lowered his arm. Kearns exhaled heavily.

They'd inched their way from his room in the direction of the elevator, but before they'd made it there'd been a ping, the doors of the elevator car had slid open and six patrolmen had been disgorged from within. He and Kearns had barely enough time to duck down a side passage while the officers passed. Normally any cops who spotted him wouldn't stand a chance, but in his current condition Herron wasn't sure he would. Being caught would end Kearns' career and his freedom.

"Let's go." Herron wrapped his arm around her

neck again and pushed off the wall. He was happy to let her lead the escape. She knew the building and his head was still foggy.

She put a hand on his chest, a silent command to stop, and left him resting against a wall while she moved ahead to scout out their path. When she returned, the gloomy expression on her face told him all he needed to know. The elevator was a no-go zone now. Without waiting for his input, she led him back towards his room, then past it to the stairs. Short of an assault rifle or an invisibility cloak, they were the next best option.

Herron was surprised to find the cops weren't guarding the stairwell, but he'd take the break. It was slow going, Herron's physical condition making the stairs exponentially harder than walking on a flat surface, but Kearns did her best to help him walk. They took it one step at a time, moving with glacial speed but gradually making progress.

He expected the police to burst into the stairwell and overwhelm them at any moment; instead he and Kearns made it safely down one floor, then two, then more. As they neared the bottom of the building, Herron started to believe they might make it. He didn't know what Kearns had planned to get them out of the building itself, but so far so good.

By the time they reached the ground floor, Herron was sweating from the exertion and short of breath. He hated being so sapped of strength and needed to rest. He leaned heavily against the wall, closed his eyes and took several long breaths. Kearns kept hold of him the whole time, clearly worried he was going to fall again.

After they'd rested for a little while, her look of concern softened and she helped him off the wall. "Ready?"

"Yep." Herron grunted with the effort of taking his own weight again. "What's the plan?"

"It's all fine." She smiled. "We hit the parking garage and get you out of here. Follow me."

Herron frowned: her plan couldn't be as simple as she suggested. He had flashbacks to the last time they'd had to escape the CDC building – that time he'd had to best two security guards.

Wrapped up again in their strange embrace, they continued down the final flight of stairs to the basement. He'd hoped he'd be feeling better by now, but he was still as weak as a newborn. As Kearns opened the door to the parking garage, Herron propped himself against a wall once more to catch his breath.

Kearns peeped out into the carpark and smiled. "All clear. Now we just need to get to my car."

With agonizing slowness, they headed into the dim open area beyond the stairs. Every parking space was full, which suggested it was the middle of the work day. They made it down one row of cars and were about to move into the second, when the sound of heavy footfalls behind them made Herron freeze.

He turned awkwardly and came face-to-face with a cop.

\* \* \*

"Hold it right there!" The cop shouted and aimed his pistol at Herron, only glancing at Kearns for only a split-second. "Ma'am, step away from him."

"If she steps away from me I'll fall." Herron wrapped his arm tighter around Kearns' shoulder and she did the same with her arm around his waist. "What's the plan, officer?"

"You get on the ground and don't move an inch while I call for backup." The patrolman's voice was hard and uncompromising – about forty years old, he was a grizzled veteran who'd no doubt seen his share of violence. "You do something contrary to that, I shoot you."

Herron raised an eyebrow. "You know we're in the Center for Disease Control, right? You see how weak I am? You think that's the flu?"

Kearns tensed as she realized where he was going with this. "My patient has a virus. It's weaponized smallpox, basically. I'm transporting him to another facility for treatment."

"My orders are to arrest a man who looks a lot like you." The cop's aim didn't waver. "Now slowly step away from the woman, get on the ground and don't move."

"The only way you're going to stop me is by shooting me. That'll mean blood. And like the doctor here said, I've got one of the deadliest viruses in human history." He kept his breathing shallow. Kearns had told him he was cured, but the cop didn't know that. "Do you have a wife? Kids?"

The cop's aim wavered, his arms shaking ever so slightly, and his eyes darted to Kearns. When she nodded, the policeman took a step back. Herron didn't need to be psychic to know what was going through his head: was forty grand annual salary worth the risk of a horrible death?

The patrolman was teetering. He just needed one final push.

"Nobody will ever know if you let us go." Kearns smiled at the officer. "Please, it harms nobody."

"It harms me!" The cop scoffed. "There're cameras all over this building. If I let you go, I'll lose my job. I lose my job, I lose my family…"

"I've taken care of that."

Both Herron and the cop turned towards the voice. A bookish-looking man was walking slowly in their direction with his hands held out. He grinned at Erica and Herron sensed her tensing beside him. The cop turned and aimed the pistol at the newcomer, whose good humor evaporated. He stopped in his tracks and put his hands up higher, fear painted on his face.

"Everyone calm down." There was an edge to Kearns' voice. "This's Christopher. He works here in IT. He's making sure we don't show up on any cameras."

Christopher nodded, clearly terrified now the attention was focused on him. "All anyone is seeing is a test pattern. There's not even a recording."

Herron knew it was time to act. The longer they waited the more chance there was of a new arrival or frayed nerves upsetting the balance and all this ending in tragedy. He looked at the cop. "There'll be no consequences for anyone if we walk away. Nobody will ever know you found me. But if you press the issue we all lose."

The cop lowered his weapon and slipped it into its holster. "Get out of here."

Only when the cop had backed away and exited the parking garage did Herron exhale. He turned to Kearns. "Time to go."

She led him to a new model black Audi, Christopher trailing behind them. Herron was at least strong enough not to need the stranger to carry him the way Kearns had. He headed for the driver's door, but Kearns blocked his way, a faint smile on her face. He looked at her and frowned.

She smiled. "Really? In your condition?"

Herron gave a short laugh, relented and walked

around to the passenger side. Kearns unlocked the car and said something to him, but her words were lost; all his focus was consumed by his reflection in the car window.

It was the first time he'd seen his appearance since climbing out of bed and it wasn't a positive experience.

His eyes were bloodshot and sunken. His hair was longer than usual and he was sporting a scraggly beard. When added to his physical weakness and the fog still shrouding his mind, it was clear his treatment at the CDC had been hard on his body.

Kearns seemed to read his mind. "We'll get you cleaned up soon enough. Get in. We don't have a lot of time."

Herron opened the door and climbed into the car, expecting Kearns to do the same. Instead, she stood close to Christopher, sharing a few moments of conversation with him, then a brief embrace. They separated, and as Christopher headed back to the stairs, Kearns got into the car and started it.

Herron looked at her. "What now?"

She smiled. "It's all taken care of."

## 2

HERRON WOKE WITH A START, sighed and rubbed his face. A glance at his alarm clock showed it was lunchtime, long past time to get up, but even so he hadn't slept much. Like most nights, his dreams had been filled with the faces of the dead, grotesque reminders of Herron's career as a paid killer. Every one of them had deserved their death, but whenever Herron closed his eyes, he was locked up with them in the cell of his mind. And it was a life sentence.

He threw off the covers and climbed out of bed. The early morning sun was peeking through the blinds, but there was no warmth. The hardwood floorboards were icy under his feet and a chill ripple through him: Georgia was cold this time of year, but despite the temperature, Herron didn't bother with the farmhouse's ducted heating. Instead, he simply dressed in jeans, a t-shirt, a sweater and boots. He'd shower later.

He was halfway to the kitchen when he heard the sound of a car engine and the crunch of gravel. He froze. Only one person visited him, once a week, and today was the wrong day. He hurried to the front door, pausing only to grab his hunting rifle.

He peeked through the corner of his drawn blinds. A Toyota was pulling to a stop in the driveway – he'd never seen the car before and he couldn't make out the driver. That made the situation a potentially dangerous one. He chambered a round, opened the door and took aim at the car. Only when he saw Erica Kearns at the wheel did he lower the rifle.

He called out to her as she emerged from the vehicle. "You should've warned me you'd bought a new car."

"I borrowed it from a friend." She shrugged. "Now are you going to shoot me or pour me some coffee?"

"I don't know. I'm low on coffee." Herron smiled and gestured for her to follow him into the house.

Kearns was the only person who knew about this location. She'd helped him make it into a home after their escape from the CDC. They'd driven straight to the remote Georgia homestead and she'd announced it was his for as long as he needed it, rented using cash and with neither of their names were attached to the property. Herron trusted her, but he'd double checked the arrangements. She'd done the job properly. Not even the realtor knew who really lived on the farm.

Once he'd settled in and finished healing, Herron had tried to get in touch with his handler. He'd openly defied orders in his pursuit of the madman who'd threatened to unleash the Omega Strain, and he'd had no contact with his handler since he'd gone rogue. The phone number had been disconnected and it was clear Herron had been cut loose, his former life gone. Now, except for Kearns' weekly supply runs, he never made contact with another soul.

He wouldn't admit it to her, but her visits were the highlight of each week.

He crossed the kitchen to the coffee pot and turned it on. "What's going on at work, Erica?"

"I got promoted!" She smiled and sat down at the dining table. "They don't have a clue I helped you. Christopher did a good job on the cameras and the cop never talked. For all anyone knows, you got away on your own."

They continued the small talk as they waited for the coffee. Then, when he was sitting opposite her and they each had a mug in front of them, he waited for her to raise the usual topic – the one she brought up every time she visited. It took three sips of coffee, less time than normal.

She put her coffee down on the table and looked him straight in the eye. "I've got supplies in the car for you, but I want this to be the last time I need to bring them."

"That's fine." Herron held her gaze. "You've helped me for months. You don't owe me anything."

She sighed and leaned forward. "I owe you everything, Mitch. You're a hero, but nobody knows it. You need to rejoin civilization."

"Civilization has no place for me." Herron shrugged. "You should've left me to die in that lab. And there's no way you should've risked yourself to help me escape the CDC."

"When will you stop feeling sorry for yourself?" She put a hand on top of his. "You can't live out here like a hermit forever."

For an instant he kept his hand in place beneath hers, then he stood and walked to the fridge. "Would you like some breakfast? I've got some homemade bread."

"It's worse than I thought." A slight smile turned the edges of her lips upwards. "From international assassin to baker?"

"Do you want some or not?"

* * *

Herron waved to Kearns as she drove away in the Toyota. She'd told him she had to get to work for an afternoon meeting and he was disappointed at how brief her visit had been. He watched the car until it was a speck in the distance, then hefted the grocery bags she'd brought for him and hauled them inside.

He was halfway to the kitchen when a shrill alarm shattered the silence. He dropped the bags and ran to where his rifle was propped against the counter. After a few seconds, the high-pitched whine cut out, but the tripwire had done its job. Someone was sneaking onto the property. He just had to figure out who they were and how they'd found him.

Herron had placed the booby traps around the outskirts of the farm in the first week he'd lived there. They were small, weather-resistant, simple pieces of technology designed to send a signal to a receiver inside the house. Whoever had just set one off had been foiled by gear worth about five bucks.

Keeping low, he rushed back to the front of the house and knelt near a window. He kept his blinds drawn at all times, which forced him to rely on the skylights for illumination, but paid off in a situation like this. He pulled back a corner of the blind and peeked out. Everything seemed ordinary, the farm peaceful under the blue, cloudless sky.

Then he saw a glint in the distance.

"Fuck!"

Herron ducked. Above his head, the window shattered as a chunk of the wooden frame exploded. Herron winced as he was showered with broken glass and wood splinters. A split second later came the crack of a supersonic rifle round. Whoever had set off the tripwire was a sniper and the only reason Herron was still alive was the reflection of the sun off the rifle's scope.

When there was no immediate follow-up shot, Herron scooted along the floor and dragged his rifle to a different window. This time, he kept his head out of sight and used the tip of the rifle barrel to move the blind a little. He flinched as the window blasted inwards and an impact jerked the rifle in his hand. The shot had struck the barrel of his weapon.

"Shit." Herron tossed the rifle to the ground. It was useless now.

He retreated from the front of the house, staying down below the line of the windows. There was no way for him to win a shootout now and he couldn't rely on any help arriving. Kearns had chosen the farm for its isolation, so nobody else would've heard the shot. He was on his own.

Not that he needed help. He was used to working alone. As the sniper waited for another shot, Herron would be working to turn the tables on him.

Clear of immediate danger, he considered who might've sent the shooter. Unless Kearns had betrayed him, there was only one possibility – his former employers. The only plausible explanation was that they'd followed Kearns here, but that meant they had an interest in her as well. Herron's former masters played for keeps and now Kearns was in as much danger as he was. He had to warn her.

Crossing to the back of the house, Herron flicked a switch on the wall. There was a rumble the ducted heating and cooling system kicked in. He turned it up to full, the result like a hurricane blowing through the house. The shooter would be kept busy watching all six windows at the front of the house now, as the heating system agitated every blind. It should be enough of a distraction for Herron to escape.

He grabbed one of his go bags and took a pistol from it, then hefted the bag onto his back, pushed the door open and broke into a run away from the house. He half-expected to take a bullet. He was taking a risk by assuming there wasn't a second sniper watching the back of the house, but it was a calculated one. The fact that no shot came only confirmed to him that his former masters had sent the shooter: when he'd been in their employ, Herron had always worked alone and it appeared this assassin was doing the same.

Knowing the house would obscure the shooter's sight line while he found cover, Herron focused on speed rather than stealth. He ran for fifty yards until he reached the point where the yard turned into a field and sloped away from the house. Though he had no animals or crops, he did have plenty of land on this farm and he planned to use it.

He crawled until he was side-on to the house and able to see where the shooter had set up. Now he'd escaped containment, without the shooter knowing, his foe had blown it. In truth, the sniper had been at a disadvantage since triggering the tripwire and missing his first shots. Now the shooter would have to move in eventually and all Herron had to do was wait.

The problem was that the longer he waited, the more risk to Kearns if she was a target too. Herron had the skills to stand a chance against a trained killer, she didn't. The sooner he could head to Atlanta and make sure she was safe, the better.

Just as Herron's reserves of patience were running low, the shooter moved. A man in forest camouflage broke cover and scurried in the direction of the house: the sniper couldn't retreat without finishing the job and he'd clearly decided that waiting for another shot was a poor bet against the chance that Herron was already dead or had escaped.

If Herron still had his rifle, it'd already be over, but he only had a pistol and the range was too extreme to make a shot worthwhile. Luckily, he had a better idea.

The operative continued to close in on the house, moving quickly. Herron didn't move an inch until the would-be killer reached the porch. Only then did he reach into his bag and wrap his fingers around a remote.

A large gas tank dominated the western side of the house, holding the fuel for its diesel generator. Herron had rigged it for another purpose. He waited while the killer opened the front door and moved inside, then flipped the safety cover off the remote and pressed a button.

The explosion blew the house to matchsticks, the detonation causing Herron's ears to throb and the ground to shake underneath him. Flames licked the carcass of the property as debris showered the ground for fifty yards around and the rolling fireball became a plume of greasy smoke billowing into the sky.

There'd always been a chance Herron's former employers would come for him and rigging the gas tank to blow had been his scorched-earth option if his hideout was ever exposed. It meant most of his cash and supplies were gone as well, but he had enough in his backpack to manage.

"150," Herron murmured, adding the hitman to his tally of bodies dropped over the years. The ritual gave him perspective, ensured he never became numb to death.

As if his dreams would let him.

He stood and moved in on the house. It was burning fiercely now and small spot fires were breaking out around it. When the cops finally stumbled upon the scene, they'd find enough human remains to fill a matchbox. They'd assume the person who'd rented the place was dead and maybe even chalk it up to an accident.

Either way, Herron would be long gone.

Stuffing the pistol down the back of his jeans, he walked to his car. It was parked far enough from the house to have escaped serious damage, though it'd been showered with debris. He grabbed his spare car keys from his bag, opened the door and climbed inside. After a final glance at the devastation, he started the engine and drove away.

* * *

Herron flicked on his hazard lights and killed the engine. With 'No Parking' signs posted on Clifton Road, near the Center for Disease Control Headquarters, faking an auto emergency was the best way to watch the CDC precinct for a little while. Kearns had been headed for work when she'd left his house and now it was near the end of the work day, Herron hoped he wouldn't have to wait too long to see her car leaving. Sooner or later, a breakdown was bound to attract the attention of a passing cop.

He popped the hood of the car and got out. Then he settled in to wait, poking around at the engine with one eye on the CDC building. Within a few minutes, cars were streaming out of the basement carpark in increasing numbers – the early quitters hitting the road. Herron kept his eyes peeled for the Toyota Kearns had driven to the farm, but all he saw were unfamiliar sedans and SUVs. Nobody paid him any attention except to glance in sympathy or curiosity at his broken-down car.

Almost half an hour passed and darkness started to settle in before he spotted her vehicle. He sighed with relief. "Finally."

He slammed the hood, got in the car and was easing out into traffic moments after Kearns passed. The traffic was light, which made it easy to catch up with her. Following her, he snaked through the city onto the I-85. Herron wasn't sure where Kearns lived, but she'd commented once that she only had a thirty-minute commute. Anonymous in the endless river of red tail lights ahead of him, following Kearns was simple. Even if she was alert, she'd no way of knowing who was driving behind her.

When she turned off the highway, Herron was a couple of car lengths behind her. After two more turns, they were driving through the quiet streets of John's Creek, one of Atlanta's ritzier suburbs. Kearns slowed and turned into the driveway of an expensive-looking house. She'd never talked about her home before, but Herron could respect that. Everyone wanted to keep some parts of their lives private.

He pulled over twenty yards before he reached her house, killing the lights but leaving the engine running. He expected her to spot his vehicle, but she didn't look in his direction as she locked her car and headed to her front door. A motion-sensitive light came on, illuminating the front of the house.

Herron frowned. Something was wrong. He trusted his gut and right now it was churning like he was aboard a small boat in rough seas. He took his eyes off Kearns for a moment and looked further up the street. Nothing there. A check of his mirrors showed there was nothing behind him either.

Soon Kearns would be through her front door. Once she was inside, he could stay parked out the front and make sure she was safe. But when the door to her house opened, he froze. A man was waiting for her in the doorway, not with a weapon but... a bunch of flowers.

Kearns leaned in to kiss him.

It was Christopher, the IT guy who'd helped them escape the CDC.

Herron gripped the wheel so tight his knuckles went white. He'd saved the world with Kearns, spent months recuperating with her and having her as his only contact with the outside. Not once had she mentioned Christopher except for the brief moment in the parking garage of the CDC. Now he was a new addition to an already complex situation and even though Herron owed him a debt, he'd much rather the man was out of the picture.

As he watched them, headlights swung into the road ahead, blinding him. Herron blinked and shielded his eyes with his hand enough to see a sedan slowing as it neared Kearns' house. The two lovers standing in the doorway were oblivious to the vehicle, even as a hand appeared out of the driver's side window holding a pistol.

The shooter fired and Christopher slumped to the ground.

Herron shouted in outrage. He mightn't have relished Christopher being part of the equation, but the man *had* helped save him back at the CDC. He shifted his car into drive and floored it, aiming right at the assassin's vehicle. Kearns was easy pickings and she'd be dead in seconds unless he could do something. With his speed climbing and the distance closing, Herron flickered his lights and pounded the car horn repeatedly to distract the hitman.

"Look at me!" Herron shouted, desperate and angry. "Look at me, you bastard!"

The assassin leaned out of the driver's window enough to adjust his aim away from the house and towards the oncoming car. Herron ducked low as several rounds blew through his windshield in a tight pattern, separated by barely an inch. He let out a guttural scream and braced for impact.

The car's smooth forward acceleration ended in a violent collision that drowned out his scream. Herron was thrown forward, his seat belt crushing his chest like a kick from a horse and his forehead slamming into the airbag. Then it was all over except for the incessant droning of the other car's horn.

Herron coughed and shook his head, dizzy from the airbag's impact. As the safety device deflated, he could see his foe in the other car, similarly stunned. There was no time to waste. He grabbed his pistol from the back of his jeans and aimed it through the windshield a fraction of a second before the enemy assassin could do the same.

He put two rounds into the man's chest and one into his head. The operative slumped forward, held in place by his seat belt.

"151."

He unbuckled his seat belt and pushed the door. It was stuck, warped by the impact, but when he kicked out it groaned open on its hinges. He grabbed his bag from the passenger seat and climbed out of the car. Half the neighborhood had emerged from their homes to see what the noise was about and the cops wouldn't be far away. Herron had kept Kearns safe from the immediate threat, but they were still in danger. They had to move.

## 3

HERRON RAN across the garden to the front door, just as the first police sirens began wailing in the distance. Kearns was slumped on her knees, crying over Christopher's body, and Herron reached down to check for a pulse. There was none. Kearns looked up at him, the hope in her eyes erased by agony and fear.

Herron held his hands wide and kept his voice calm. "Erica, we have to go. We're not out of danger."

She switched her gaze between him and Christopher, tears streaking freely down her cheeks. Over her sobs, he could hear the sirens in the distance drawing closer.

"I'm here to help." His voice was more urgent this time. Christopher was gone, he couldn't change that, but he could focus on the living and deal with the situation if they left right away. "I'm sorry about Christopher, but—"

"He's dead!" She wailed. "My boyfriend is dead and it's your fault! You brought them here!"

Herron shook his head. If anything, the opposite was true: she'd led the killers to *his* doorstep. Regardless, they had to *go*. There were two bodies out front of the house and he doubted the cops would be in the mood to hear his explanation.

He crouched down and held a hand out. "They came after me, too. I came here to make sure you were safe."

She scoffed. "Why would they want me, Mitch? I'm nothing to them"

It was a good question. Herron could understand his former employers wanting his scalp. He'd disobeyed them and killed one of his own colleagues, but Kearns was completely irrelevant except for the fact she'd helped him. There were only two reasons to go after her: one was to pull him out of hiding, but they'd already done that. The other was to erase everyone associated with him.

Herron glanced over his shoulder and then looked back at her. "You need to calm down."

"Don't you *fucking* tell me to —"

"Erica, please. We're wasting time. I'm your only chance to stay alive here."

She regarded him with eyes filled with doubt and pain. At last, she nodded. "Fine."

Herron stood to his full height and held out his hand again. "Let's go."

"I need to get some things!"

He shook his head. "No time."

"My laptop, my research, I —"

Herron didn't respond. He just dragged her through to the back of the house. The police would come through the front, so the rear of the building was the best way out.

Kearns' face crumbled as reality sunk in. Once a group of international assassins was on your tail, there were no half measures – you kill, you escape or you die. She gave no further protest as Herron unlocked the back door and pushed it open.

He led Kearns to the back of her neatly manicured lawn and let go of her hand. After tossing his bag over the fence, he scaled it, then propped himself up on the other side and held a hand out to help her up. Despite the blank look on her face, she gripped his hand and he hauled her up.

Herron dropped to the ground. They were in the backyard of the neighboring property. The space was littered with the detritus of children – bikes and toys – but he could see nothing useful, so his mind kept working. He spotted the garage and smiled. Grabbing his bag, he stalked over to the outbuilding, kicked the door open and flicked the lights on.

A decked out black and chrome Harley Davidson sat in the middle of the garage. The keys were in the ignition.

Herron grinned. For the first time today, he'd had some luck.

"Ever ride on a Harley?" He turned to Kearns. He'd only been on one once before, but it'd been a memorable experience – chasing a target along California State Route 190 before putting a bullet in his skull.

She stared at him, eyes puffy from crying. "What do you think?"

"First time for everything." He straddled the bike. "Get on."

She hesitated for a moment, then threw a leg over the bike and shuffled forward. Herron started the bike and revved it hard, warming the engine. Kearns wrapped her arms around him and he tensed slightly, both at what he was feeling and what he could see in front of him. The garage's roller door was grinding open, revealing a man on the other side.

Herron kicked the stand and put the bike into gear, but by now the bike's owner was standing in front of the garage to block their escape. He was holding a baseball bat, but he didn't look like he wanted to use it. Herron drew his pistol and aimed at him. The bike's owner backed off, letting the bat fall to his side. Though he swore at Herron, he didn't move to stop him.

Herron turned to Kearns. "Dig into my bag, pull out one of the bricks of cash and throw it at this gentleman."

He kept his pistol on the bike's owner as Kearns fished out the cash and tossed it onto the ground. As the man looked down at the money – easily enough to buy another bike – Herron revved hard and hit the road.

* * *

The Harley's engine sputtered and stopped.

"That's it for the gas." Herron sighed. He could've stopped to fill up, but hadn't wanted to chance being caught on a security camera feed. As it was, the bike had taken them northwest for about an hour and now they were only a little out of Chattanooga, Tennessee. "We have to walk from here."

He and Kearns dismounted, and Herron walked the bike over to the side of the highway. She watched as he kicked the stand down, silent and clearly in shock. The adrenaline shot her body had delivered at the house would've worn off by now and, as if to prove the point, she made it only a few steps before she stopped, bent over and put her hands on her knees.

"Are you okay?" He placed a hand on her back. Reassuring people wasn't one of his strengths. "We can take some time to rest if you like."

"My boyfriend was just killed in front of me, Mitch." She looked up at him, disbelief in her eyes. "So, no, I'm not okay."

Herron felt like an ass. Since they'd left the house, he'd been so focused on making sure they survived he'd barely thought about the man who hadn't. "I'm sorry, Erica."

She nodded, squeezed her eyes shut and took a few deep breaths. "Sorry. I'm just finding this all a bit overwhelming."

"Just take it one step at a time. And the first step is survival. We've contracts on our heads now."

"I have a contract on *my* head?" Kearns shook her head. "Why? I don't understand any of this, Mitch."

Herron shrugged. "I don't know. Until I do, we have to disappear."

Her eyes widened. "I can't just move away from Atlanta. What about my job? My life?"

"You need to listen." Herron put a hand on her shoulder. "Your life is gone. Your job, house, family and friends. Gone. Any plans for the future. Gone. That's how you stay alive."

"I won't hide away forever, Mitch!" Her voice was louder this time, more insistent. "Everything that's important to me is back there."

"Then you'll die."

Her face sagged and she started to cry. Herron sighed as she stepped forward and wrapped her arms around him. After a second, he returned the hug.

After a while, her sobs lessened and she pulled away. She looked up at him, her eyes red. "I'm ready."

"Okay." He nodded and gestured with his head for her to follow.

It was a three-mile walk to the center of Chattanooga and Herron held Kearns' hand the whole way. He asked a passerby the directions to the nearest Greyhound bus station, where he bought two tickets and they boarded a bus to Nashville, a city Herron knew had a lot more to offer than country music.

\* \* \*

Herron stretched as best he could in the cramped seat of the Greyhound bus, with the seatback in front of him, Kearns' head on his shoulder and the backpack on his lap limiting his movement. No sooner had he achieved some comfort, the driver braked hard and his knee slammed into the seatback. Herron winced in pain, causing Kearns to inhale sharply and move her head off his shoulder.

She sat up straight and rubbed her face. "Sorry, did I fall asleep?"

Herron laughed. "About 10 minutes out of Chattanooga."

"Where are we?"

"Almost at Nashville." Once they got there, he'd be able to access one of the stashes he'd hidden away in storage lockers and safety deposit boxes all across the country, ready to be cracked open in an emergency. In his profession, it wasn't a question of if you needed such insurance, but when. "It's going to be okay, Erica."

She forced a smile and they settled into silence, with Herron staring out the window and Kearns dozing beside him. The traffic density increased as they got closer to the center of Nashville and a city bus edged up alongside the Greyhound. Herron's eye hovered on it for a second, considering the vehicle from front to back. It looked extremely fragile and suddenly he felt very exposed.

He nudged Kearns in the ribs with his elbow. "It's time to get off."

She stirred and grumbled. "Doesn't the bus stop right in the middle of the city?"

"Yes. That's why we have to get off now. Less predictable means less vulnerable."

Herron stood, threw his backpack over one shoulder and walked down the aisle to the front of the bus. The other passengers watched him curiously, but he was focused only on the driver, who didn't even acknowledge him and kept his eyes on the road.

Herron leaned in close to the bus driver. "Any chance of stopping the bus a few blocks from the station?"

The driver kept his attention straight ahead. "We're arriving in a minute, you can get off at the same place as everyone else."

Herron pulled out his wallet and opened it. He

counted out some bills and when he reached two hundred dollars he put the small stack in the driver's cup holder. Without even glancing at the cash, the driver signaled and pulled the bus over to the side of the road. The doors opened with a hiss.

"Thanks." Herron started down the steps, with Kearns behind him.

They watched as the engine of the bus roared and it eased back onto the road. They were only two blocks away from the scheduled stop, but Herron felt safer now. As an assassin, he'd always exploited patterns and routines in the lives of his targets, so he was determined not to give anyone hunting him the same edge.

Kearns was shivering in the chill night air, her thin blouse clearly inadequate. "Are you warm enough?"

"I'm fine."

"Take this." Herron removed his sweater, held it out for her and waited while she pulled it on. It was too large, but it'd do the job.

Farther up the road, there was a boom.

Herron turned to search for the source of the explosion. The bus they'd been on a moment ago had been blown apart. Standing at a red light, it burned fiercely all along its length, its passengers certainly dead. Kearns' scream was lost in the roar of the high-powered motorbike Herron spotted zooming away down a side street. He'd have bet a lot of money that the rider had blown up the bus and now thought his targets were dead.

Members of the public were emerging from cars, houses and businesses, rushing to the bus and the doomed souls within, but forced back by the fury of the flames. Kearns too stumbled toward the bus, but Herron gripped her arm, halted her.

She pulled against his grip. "We have to help them!"

"They're dead." Herron gripped tighter until she stopped resisting, then wrapped an arm around her and led her away from the blazing bus.

"How'd they find us?" Tears streaked down Kearns' cheeks. "You said we'd be safe."

"I don't know. A CCTV feed or a traffic camera, most likely." He stopped for a moment. "Did you bring your phone with you?"

"No."

"Anything electronic?" He was kicking himself for not checking sooner. He wasn't used to being on the run. It was a rookie mistake.

"Just this." Kearns lifted her arm and showed him her watch.

"An Apple Watch?" Herron seized her arm. "They tracked us using its GPS."

"They can do that?" Kearns' eyes widened.

Herron unbuckled the watch from her wrist and glanced at the traffic ambling along Belmont Boulevard. After a few seconds, he spotted a pickup truck with an uncovered bed. He stuck his tongue out the side of his mouth and threw the watch toward the pickup. It sailed high and landed true, falling out of sight in the back of the vehicle. Soon, it'd be miles away, giving whoever was tracing Kearns a false read.

But that didn't mean they were safe. They still had to move. Herron stepped out into the street and hailed a cab.

## 4

"JUST STOP UP HERE FOR A SECOND." Herron leaned forward to talk to the cab driver and then winced as the taxi cut off another car and darted across two lanes.

Kearns gasped and gripped his hand as the cab stopped outside the Midtown Hills Police Precinct station. It was a large, uninspiring brick structure, with stairs leading up to the main door. A few cops were on the steps chatting and they stopped to stare as the taxi pulled in.

Herron turned in his seat to face Kearns. "This's your stop."

"What?" She let go of his hand, confused. "I don't understand."

"Go inside and wait. You'll be safe here until I come back."

Her eyes searched his face, as if hoping for more

of an explanation, but none came. He wouldn't leave her alone for longer than necessary, but it was too dangerous to be together until he had the resources he needed. The assassin who'd blown up the bus could still be on their tail and Herron had more chance of taking him on if he was alone. He'd get his stash, collect her and take them into hiding.

At last, she unbuckled her seat belt and leaned over to hug him. "Stay safe. I didn't bring you back from the dead only to lose you now."

Herron squeezed her tight. "If they ask why you're hanging around, tell them you're afraid and need somewhere safe to sit."

She broke the hug and frowned at him. "You damn well better come back for me, Mitch."

Herron waited while she opened the cab door, got out and climbed the steps to the station. He watched until she was inside, then looked at the cabbie. "Let's go."

They arrived at Green Hills Shopping Mall only a few minutes later. It was on the small side as far as American malls went, focusing on premium designer stores for its middle-class shoppers, but it had exactly what he needed. As soon as the cab came to a stop, he handed the driver a small wad of cash and got out.

Once inside the mall, he rushed past other shoppers and made a beeline for the entrance to a maintenance hallway. He pushed open the door and stalked down the corridor, around a corner, past an empty break room, a firefighting station and assembly point, and a pin board covered in staff notices. At last he arrived at a wall of lockers. In one of them he'd find his stash.

After finding the right locker, he looked around to make sure he was alone, then input the code and cracked open the door. He smiled. Everything was exactly as he'd left it – bricks of cash wrapped in plastic, a lunch container full of fake identification, a set of bump keys, a silenced pistol, ammunition and a cheap backpack to carry it all. Though he already had a pistol and some cash in the bag he was carrying, this was the mother lode.

"Jackpot."

Relief washed over him as he opened the backpack and stuffed the contents of the locker into it. He'd made sure only to stash what could be carried easily in the bag, so when he was finished the backpack was full and the locker was empty, except for the pistol. He loaded it and stuffed it down the back of his jeans. It was a superior weapon to the one he'd brought with him from the farm, so he tossed the old pistol into the locker and slammed the door closed. Then, after checking around one last time, he retraced his steps back to the maintenance hallway entrance.

He was almost there when he turned a corner and found himself staring down the barrel of a pistol. The man aiming it at him was smiling, the expression contrasting strangely with the deep, puckered scar that ran from the edge of his left eye down to the corner of his mouth.

Herron pulled up short. He wouldn't be able to reach his pistol before the gunman shot him, so he did the only thing he could. "Who're you?"

The man chuckled, cold and humorless. His pistol didn't move an inch. "You can call me Shade. Hand over your weapon."

Herron froze in place. The second he handed his pistol over he was a dead man. "You realize you're the third assassin I've dealt with today?"

"And the last." Shade raised an eyebrow. "Now, let's be professional about this. The pistol and the bag"

Herron had no choice. He reached behind his back, gripped the pistol and slid it along the ground. It was over, Herron knew. He'd been moments away from springing free with his stash, only to be tripped up at the final hurdle. Kearns, too; she might be safe in the police station for a while, but the assassins wouldn't stop chasing her. Hell, Shade would probably go straight for her once he'd finished here.

Shade smiled and picked up the pistol. The killer kept one pistol aimed at Herron while he ejected the magazine from the other. Keeping his weapon trained on Herron, he reached behind him and locked the door to the maintenance corridor before putting his pistol in the waistband of his jeans.

Herron was astounded. The assassin had the drop on him... was he now giving him a chance?

The cruel smile returned to Shade's face as he assumed a fighting stance. "Now... It's time for a lesson in humility."

\* \* \*

Herron raised his fists as Shade advanced. The narrow hallway would constrain their movement and wasn't the ideal place for hand-to-hand combat, but it gave Herron a chance with the pistols out of play. Though Herron didn't know how proficient his foe was, Shade's fighting stance and sadistic grin suggested he wouldn't like the answer.

"You should've just shot me. You've made this harder for yourself." Herron feigned a jab once Shade was in range and followed it home with a straight kick.

Shade took one step to the side and one step in, delivering a sharp blow to Herron's stomach. "I don't think it's harder. But it's definitely more enjoyable."

Herron coughed in pain and backed away, rattled. His foe had landed the first blow too easily and he fought to get his guard back up before Shade could capitalize. He needn't have bothered. The assassin was clearly in no hurry. He was smirking, assessing Herron the way a hawk might a field mouse.

Herron inched his way back. "Why have you been ordered to take me down?"

Shade's smile vanished. He tilted his head to the side, a curious look on his face. "Are you serious? You left the fold and went rogue. That can't go unpunished."

Herron held his ground now as Shade stepped forward. His opponent struck twice and Herron fended him off, but the moment he tried to go on the offensive his enemy stepped inside the blow and delivered a brutal elbow strike to his chin. Herron grunted, saw stars and staggered back. But Shade didn't press the advantage.

"You're a fool." The scarred killer taunted him. "You had the best job in the world. You were an avenging angel. If you played by the rules, nobody could touch you and nothing was off limits. Turning your back on us insults your handler and the entire brotherhood. That's why I'm not just going to kill you. I'm going to humiliate and dismantle you."

Herron shook his head to clear it. "You sure talk a lot."

"So my targets tell me. I think it's a sign that I enjoy my work too much. Alas, we all have a weakness." Shade shrugged, mockingly. "You, on the other hand, can't fight for shit. I don't know how you tallied up so many kills. It certainly wasn't your martial prowess."

Herron refused to rise to Shade's bait. Spitting

blood, he resumed his fighting stance. He'd never taken so many serious licks in a fight, not with his opponent making it seem so easy. It unnerved him. His best attempts to fight the other man weren't working, but with no weapons and no obvious escape, he had to try something else to best Shade. If not, this would be over very quickly.

Herron lowered his head and charged. Shade clearly wasn't expecting such an unconventional and amateur move, which was exactly why Herron did it. He tackled Shade in the midriff and took them both to the ground. Landing on top of the hitman, Herron connected with several blows before taking a fist to the solar plexus and an elbow to the cheek. The impacts sent him reeling and he fell to the ground.

"He has some fight after all!" Shade chuckled as he shuffled away from Herron. "Maybe if the hired killer business doesn't work out, you could try pro wrestling."

Herron was upright first and readied to press his brief advantage, but Shade thrust both of his hands out and a pair of small blades flew from them – one high, one low. Herron had barely time to react. He ducked low enough that the first throwing knife only glanced off his forehead, but the other embedded itself in his thigh. He grunted in pain.

"Okay, playtime is over." Back on his feet now, Shade reached into his pocket and produced a small, nasty-looking flick knife.

Something cold uncoiled in Herron's stomach. Even with an untrained foe, defending against a knife-wielding man without a blade of your own was a tricky proposition. Against a killer as skilled as Shade, who'd already bested Herron convincingly without a weapon, it was a fatal disadvantage.

Herron played defense as Shade advanced. He used his forearms to deflect Shade's first probing thrust, aimed right at his eyes, but the strikes kept coming. Herron slowly gave ground and it took every ounce of his ability and effort to stop Shade from landing a killing blow. And with each thrust, Shade laughed and taunted and mocked him.

Over and over Shade thrust the blade at him, forcing him to weave and block and make sacrifices – small nicks and cuts – to avoid a slashed artery or critical stab wound. He was giving ground and eventually one of the slices would get through.

He only had one chance.

Herron aimed a straight kick at Shade. Although fended away, the move allowed him to put some distance between them. In one smooth motion, Herron backed away one more step, until he was level with the firefighting station he'd passed earlier. He grabbed an extinguisher from the wall and pulled the pin. Shade was too slow to stop him, his eyes widening as he realized his mistake.

Herron sprayed a plume of carbon dioxide in Shade's face, then turned and ran. The knife wound in his thigh was a problem, but he'd have to cope with the pain. He cut left down an intersecting hallway as Shade fired blind behind him, the pistol rounds pounding into the wall where he'd been standing a second earlier. Sprinting down the hallway he reached a door and barged through it onto the mall's main concourse.

As the door swung closed behind him, he heard a furious shout.

"I'll find you!"

\* \* \*

Herron staggered through crowds of shoppers, who stared at his bloody and sweaty form as if he were some kind of leper. He didn't stop for a second – he needed to get away from Shade and hiding amongst the shops and shoppers in his state was going to be impossible. His only chance was to get out of the mall and into a vehicle.

He was still overwhelmed by the total dominance Shade had enjoyed over him. Herron had never been matched by anyone. It had never even been close. But in the maintenance corridor he'd met a foe so confident he'd been able to toy with Herron, taking his time to take him apart with blade and bare hands. If not for Shade's overconfidence giving him that small opening to escape...

He took a left and ran through the food court. As

he looked for an exit, there was a sudden cacophony of beeps and rings and tinny music, and every one of the diners either looked down or reached for their bags or into their pockets.

All the cell phones in the food court were ringing at once.

Herron slowed to a stop. Since waking up on the farm this morning, he'd experienced a lot of firsts. He'd been attacked by three of his former colleagues, bested by one of them, and now every phone within earshot was going crazy. Focused as he was on escaping and getting back to Kearns, the phenomenon still sent a ripple down his spine.

There was a tap on his shoulder: a woman of about 40 was holding a cell phone out to him, a look of concern on her face. "Is your name Herron?"

He gaped at her. "Yes."

"I think it's for you. They said it's a matter of life and death." From the way she was staring at him, she believed it.

Herron took the phone and immediately the others stopped ringing. He put the handset to his ear. "Hello?"

The voice that answered was electronically distorted. "You need to listen to me, Mitch. I can help to get you out. There's more than one operative on your tail, I'm watching you all on the mall CCTV."

Herron glanced up and around – several security cameras were aimed down at the food court. His shroud of anonymity had been thrown off. "How do you know my name? Who's this?"

"Forget all that. The Enclave wants to kill you, but I can get you out safe and tell you how they're finding you."

If there was more than one assassin on his tail, it changed everything. Shade had been more than enough to handle. "How do I know I can trust you?"

"Without my help, you're a dead man. That's all the trust you need." The distorted voice paused for a second. "After I get you out, I want you to meet with me."

Herron considered the offer for a second, then nodded. He'd nothing to lose. "Okay. What do I do?"

"There's an exit to your left. It's clear on the other side. Take it and head to the parking garage."

Herron dipped a hand into his backpack and tossed the woman who'd given him the phone some notes – probably enough to buy four phones – then hustled. He was running blind, with no choice but to take the caller's word for it. With multiple assassins on his tail, he needed all the help he could get. True to the caller's word, he made it to the carpark untouched. He crouched down next to a car and looked behind him. There was no sign of Shade or anyone else trying to kill him.

Herron held the phone to his ear. "Where do I go now? You better not be wasting my time."

"You're alive, aren't you? Now shut up and focus."

"Okay." Herron took a deep breath. "Wait, what do I call you?"

There was a pause. "Moses. Now cross the aisle and move three cars to your right."

Despite the situation, Herron laughed inwardly. The irony of being guided to safety by Moses, who'd parted the Red Sea, wasn't lost on him. He moved as he'd been instructed, keeping low as he crossed the aisle and moved three cars along to the right.

He stopped. A man was standing by the hood of the car, facing away from him and speaking on a cell phone. There was a bulge in the small of his back, where his shirt just covered his chinos.

"Take him out." Moses delivered a death sentence devoid of emotion. "Quickly."

Herron put the phone in his pocket and advanced – low and slow – until he was standing behind his target. As soon as he finished his call, Herron struck, placing a hand over the man's mouth and pulling back. His foe tried to break free, but Herron already had his pistol. He pressed the weapon into the man's back and fired several times, the silenced weapon making very little sound.

It was over in three seconds. Herron stepped back, letting the corpse flop to the ground. He crouched low and put the phone back to his ear. "He's down."

"I saw. Nice work. There's a car up ahead I can start remotely..." Moses' voice trailed off. "Shit. That guy you tangled with in the corridor earlier? He's heading straight for you."

Herron's eyes widened. Though he now had a pistol, he wasn't keen to meet Shade again so soon. "Get me out of here."

"Up three rows, you'll hit a Ford configured for remote start. I'll hack in, unlock it and get it moving. But you need to get to it."

He pocketed the phone again and crossed one aisle without incident, then another. He paused in front of a large SUV and peeked into the third aisle. A Ford pickup was waiting. It beeped and its taillights flashed as Moses unlocked it, followed a second later by its engine starting. Herron eased his head around the car for a look.

"It's him!" The distorted voice screamed in his ear. "Duck!"

Herron hit the deck as shots pounded into the SUV. "Fuck!"

"Found you!" Shade's shout came from a few aisles behind him.

"Get out of there, Mitch!" The distorted voice was excited now. "You can't beat him!"

Herron thought about standing and shooting at Shade, but the voice had been right so far. He darted across to the Ford, opened the door, tossed his backpack onto the passenger seat and climbed inside. He slammed the door shut, shifted into reverse and backed the Ford out as quick as he could before popping into drive and flooring it.

The pickup took a beating as Shade fired on it, shots pounding into panels and shattering windows. Tires squealing, the vehicle gained speed. Herron gritted his teeth, expecting an explosion of pain, but it never came.

The shots stopped. Shade was probably out of ammo. Herron let out a whoop of joy and sat up as the pickup roared to the end of the aisle. He tapped the brakes, turned and headed for the exit.

He caught sight of Shade for only a second: the killer had a snarl on his face.

Herron smiled. "Next time, fucko."

As he pulled onto the road, racing for the police station where he'd left Kearns, he put the phone to his ear again. "I'm clear."

"I saw." Moses breathed heavily. "If you want to know why they're chasing you and how to stop it, meet me in Baltimore at 7:00 PM tomorrow. Alone."

"When and where?"

Moses recited an address and then hung up. Herron tossed the phone out the window. He was shaken by the ease in which the string of hit men had tracked him to Nashville, and now this Moses was offering the answers he needed; he had no choice but to meet. But first he had to get a new car, a change of clothes and reunite with Kearns.

Then the hard work would begin.

## 5

HERRON STIFLED a yawn as he switched the windshield wipers to their highest setting. The blades cut across the rain that had pounded the car constantly since they'd crossed the border to Maryland. If nothing else, the incessant hammering was keeping him awake. The noise had no such effect on Kearns – she was sleeping soundly in the passenger seat, but that just meant Herron had to answer fewer questions.

It also gave him space to think.

He hadn't realized how much the events at the shopping mall had rocked his confidence until his mind and body had relaxed a little. After stealing a car and some clothes from a gym bag he'd found in the trunk, Herron had picked up Kearns from the police station. By the time they began their drive to Baltimore, his hands had started to shake. He'd got it under control quickly, but the sensation was something he'd never experienced before.

The advantage Shade had over him had been absolute. Herron couldn't beat the man and wasn't convinced he could escape him, either, so getting answers from Moses in Baltimore became all-important. Herron hoped at the very least he'd learn why his former employers were after them and perhaps get the information he needed to make them stop.

After driving for another five minutes, he decided they needed to eat before their rendezvous. He waited for the next exit sign, signaled and turned off the highway.

Beside him, Kearns stretched in her seat, straightening her whole body like a cat and then sitting up tall. "Did I fall asleep?"

"About ten minutes out of Nashville." Herron laughed. "I'm going to stop so we can get some gas and some food."

She caught sight of a destination sign amidst the fury of the storm. "Frederick, Maryland?"

"Got something against the place?" Herron smiled. "It's home to the National Museum of Civil War Medicine."

"You read that on a sign." She sighed. "Anyway, don't tell me we're here for that."

Herron didn't respond and she didn't push the

issue. He hadn't told her the plan. He wasn't sure she'd be in favor of it.

He pulled them off the highway and parked at the first fast-food restaurant he saw – a McDonalds. "You're going to need to decide if a burger is worth getting wet for."

"Sure is." She unbuckled her seat belt and then started to remove the sweater he'd given her after they'd got off the Greyhound bus.

Herron frowned. "What're you doing?"

"Keeping us dry."

She opened the door and was met with the full force of the rain. She climbed out of the vehicle and ran around to his door with the sweater held over her head. Despite the makeshift umbrella, the storm was ferocious and she was soaked by the time she was half-way around the car. Her white blouse was sticking to her, her bra visible through it, and her black pants were soaked.

Herron popped his door open. "You're crazy!"

Herron got out, slipped one arm around her waist and carried his bag in the other. He kicked the car door closed and they headed for the entry, squeezed in close to one another. Once they were under the awning, Kearns lowered the sweater and they separated. Her attempt to stay dry had failed miserably and they were both laughing.

"I wonder if they have paper towels? Christopher

used to –" Her smile vanished and she froze in place as her memory caught up with her.

"Come on." Herron took her hand, squeezed it, and led her inside.

They walked to the counter – dripping water all the way – and ordered. When their food was ready, they carried it to the furthest table from the door. Herron threw the backpack into the booth and took a seat with his back to the wall, so he could see the entire restaurant. Kearns sat opposite him.

They ate in silence for a few minutes, before Herron decided it was time to spill the beans. "Erica, we're headed to Baltimore to meet up with someone. He's promised to tell us why the assassins are after us."

She frowned. "You told me we were going to hide once you had the money. You said that's how we'd stay safe."

"I know. I was wrong." He sighed. "At the Mall, one of them almost took me down. The price of getting out of the situation there was agreeing to meet in Baltimore."

Kearns' face clouded over and she put her food down. She clearly wasn't impressed by the change of plan, but Herron was surprised by the strength of resolve on her face. He shouldn't have been: over their time together he'd come to expect a certain strength from her.

"Mitch, I don't want to run all over America

chasing after killers." Kearns reached out and placed a hand on his. "I came with you because you said we'd hide and be safe."

He nodded. "I know, I—"

"Let me finish." She squeezed his hand. "I've lost my career, my boyfriend and my home. I trust you, but I'm not racing back into danger."

Herron sat back. He wanted to keep her close and to protect her, but it was possible staying close to him would be even more dangerous than splitting up. He could go to the meeting in Baltimore, follow that path for as long as it went, then return to her when things were safer.

He nodded. She'd made her choice and he respected it. He dug into his backpack and, after looking around to make sure nobody was watching, he switched some of the contents into the newly emptied McDonalds food bag – a quarter of the cash, the bump keys, the identification and the few magazines of spare ammo. Then he put the backpack on the floor between them and took another gulp of his soda.

"The bag under the table has enough money to cover you for a while. Stay here. It's still dangerous in Atlanta and the less you move around, the safer you'll be. Once I get some more answers and I'm sure I can keep us safe, I'll come back for you."

"I understand." She put her other hand on his,

squeezed it tight for several long seconds. "Just come back to me, Mitch."

* * *

Herron parked the car on level five of the parking garage and killed the engine, as he'd been instructed. After separating from Kearns at the McDonalds, he'd driven the final hour to Baltimore. With plenty of time to spare before the meeting, he'd caught some patchy sleep on the back seat of the car then surveilled the parking garage. He'd spotted nothing of note, so now he was waiting with the pistol in his lap and watching the car's clock tick to 7:00 PM.

On the stroke of seven, the lights in the parking garage cut out completely.

"Damn it." Herron's night vision was shot and there was no natural light at all in the enclosed space.

He turned on the car's lights and then climbed out, holding his pistol. The throaty roar of powerful engines echoed off the concrete and soon he was surrounded by three boxy, black SUVs. The occupants of each vehicle climbed out, all wearing balaclavas and aiming silenced weapons at him. He was outnumbered and outgunned, so did the only sensible thing and tossed his pistol onto the ground.

"Thanks for coming, Mitch." One of them spoke with a distorted voice. "I'm Moses. It's time for a ride."

Herron nodded and held his hands out wide. He

didn't resist as they rushed in and restrained his arms with plasticuffs, but grunted as they forced a hood over his head and shoved him forward. He tried to soak up as much information about his captors as he could, but without his eyesight, it was difficult. All he had was that they drove near-identical vehicles, wore near-identical clothing and moved with precision.

He was taken to the back seat of one of the SUVs and forced inside. With a sigh, Herron made himself as comfortable as he could while still wearing a hood and cuffs and counted down the time until the SUV stopped. Less than an hour after he'd been shoved into the vehicle, the door opened again and he was dragged out roughly.

Herron snarled underneath the hood. "I'm not resisting, but if you keep up this up I might just start."

One of his captors snorted and gave Herron a hard shot to the stomach. The blow drove the wind out of him and doubled him over in pain. Whoever these guys were, they could throw a punch.

They forced him into a chair, secured his limbs with cable ties and cinched a rope around his waist. When he was fully restrained, the hood was ripped from his head and he was overwhelmed by light. He closed his eyes against it. "You know how to make a guy feel welcome."

"You're lucky to be alive at all."

It was a female voice. Herron squinted and after his vision had adjusted was able to see a woman in black fatigues was standing in front of him. She was in her mid-thirties, lean and with hard facial features topped off with a messy brown ponytail. She was holding a submachine gun she looked very comfortable with.

"Moses?" Herron's surprise was obvious.

She flashed him a look of disdain. "You expected a man?"

Herron shrugged and looked around. He was in a cavernous, near-empty warehouse – except for the chair he was seated in, the dark SUVs and his black-clad captors there was very little to see. Joining the woman – Moses – were four others, all men and all about the same age as her. Herron still had no idea who he was dealing with, but he suspected he was about to find out.

Moses stepped forward. "Thanks for trusting me, Mitch. I know coming here was a risk for you."

Herron gave a bitter laugh. "Some welcome. I—"

She held up a hand. "You need to understand it's as much a risk for us. We're also being hunted. That's why we're dealing with you carefully."

The revelation took Herron off guard and he fell back on thick sarcasm to hide his surprise. "You better watch out. Once I get out of these restraints I'll deal with you all."

One of the men shook his head and stepped forward, aiming his submachine gun at Herron.

"This's a waste of time. Let's blow him away and get out of here."

Herron smiled at the new player, his eyes ice-cold, but the loudmouth's attention was on the woman now, and vice versa. Some sort of silent battle of wills was in progress. She was clearly their leader, but her authority was being challenged. The loudmouth stepped back begrudgingly. She'd won.

Having stared down her subordinate, Moses turned back to Herron. "Sorry. I hope that little display won't dissuade you from working with us."

"Working with you?" Herron snorted. "I came here for answers. Once I have them, I'm gone."

"Answers?" She smiled thinly. "Well then, it's time for you to learn about the Enclave."

* * *

Herron frowned. *The Enclave? What the fuck is the Enclave?* "I don't know what you're talking about."

Moses pulled a chair up opposite him and sat. "It's key to everything. The Enclave is your former employer. Our former employer. They're the ones trying to kill us."

Herron frowned. "Why di—"

"Why'd they wait several months before attacking you and your lady friend?" Moses stole the words from his mouth. "Because of us. We decided we'd had enough and took the fight to them. Now they're reacting and anyone who's out is *out*. We started a war and you're caught in it. You're collateral damage."

She got to her feet, stepped behind him and slashed the restraints that were binding his limbs to the chair. He moved his arms and legs as she went to work on the rope that was around his waist, but kept the motions slow and easy. There were still four trained killers aiming firearms at him.

Moses paced around in front of him again. "You've got the chance to join us and help stop them."

"No, thanks." Herron stood up. "It's nice to know the name of who's after me, but going to war against them doesn't help me stay safe."

"You're wrong. The Enclave doesn't just order the deaths of... bad people." Moses' tone had changed now he was free. "They take out terrorists and they stage terror attacks. They kill child murderers and they kill children. They do whatever they need to for maximum profit. Do you think you'll be safe if we don't stop them? Do you think Kearns will?"

Herron ignored her. He wanted no part of this. "Where's my gun and my money? I don't appreciate having my stuff stolen."

Moses reached behind her back, grabbed his pistol and held it out to him. "Your money is gone."

Herron snorted as he took the pistol and stuffed it down the back of his jeans. "Liars *and* thieves."

"There's only a few of us who can stop them, Mitch."

"None of my business. Good luck."

He turned and headed for the exit – no one tried to stop him.

It had been a mistake to come here. He should've stayed with Kearns and relied on his own skills and wits. Now he was more committed than ever that they needed to disappear. He had his gun and his freedom. He'd figure out the rest.

But Moses' words nagged at him. Everything he'd ever achieved in his profession and all the risks he'd taken had rested on the knowledge that he was killing people who deserved it. Now Moses was asking him to believe his former employers killed the good and the bad indiscriminately. Herron wasn't sure it was true – he *was* certain, however, that he was now a rogue player in between two frighteningly powerful factions.

Lost in thought, he almost missed the dull thud of something pounding against the door. It swung inwards and a pair of small grenades skidded across the floor.

"They're here!"

His words were drowned out by the flashbang grenades. Though he was about ten feet from the devices and outside their optimum area of effect, he still lost his hearing and succumbed to sickening dizziness. Thankfully, he had enough experience with flashbangs to quickly overcome their effects. He aimed and fired twice at the doorway, just as the first attacker stepped through it.

"Unh." The newcomer grunted as both shots took him in the chest and he fell.

The rest of the breach team pushed in and Moses and her crew opened fire. The carnage gave Herron a chance to get to cover behind one of the SUVs – he took a second to recover, then stood up high enough to aim his pistol over the hood.

It was chaos.

The breach team had downed one of Moses' men, but they'd taken several casualties in return and their cohesion was shot to hell.

Herron fired and downed two attackers in quick succession, then ducked as return fire pounded the SUV. His hearing had returned enough that he made out the dull thud of submachine gun rounds hitting the bodywork, as well as the occasional deep boom of a 12-gauge shotgun. If he popped his head up it'd get shot off. Instead, he lay on his side and fired off his last shots under the vehicle, taking down one more attacker in the legs.

Out of ammo, his eyes widened as an attacker rounded the back of the SUV and aimed a shotgun at him. Herron stared at the man's hand as his finger pulled back on the trigger, the moment passing in slow motion as he waited for the end.

It never came.

There was a flat 'pop' and the gunman was a

bloody mess on the floor. Time sped up again. Herron looked behind him. Moses was crouched behind one of the other SUVs and had enjoyed a perfect line of sight for the shot that had saved his life. She flashed a smile, shifted her aim and got back to work.

Herron scampered over to the shotgun and pried it out of the man's dead hands. A shell was already loaded, so he climbed to his feet and leveled the barrel, searching for a target. He was too late. The final attacker was just falling to the ground. The entire 10-man breach team was down, dead or incapacitated.

Herron stood to his full height and rounded the SUV, sweeping the barrel of the shotgun between the wounded men to make sure nobody tried anything "We need to go."

"This safe house is blown." Moses said, and pointed at the SUVs, silently ordering her remaining men to mount up. Then she looked back at Herron. "Are you coming with us or not?"

Herron shrugged. "For now."

## 6

HERRON STIRRED as the car slowed to a stop. He rubbed his face and looked at Moses. "What time is it?"

"2:00 AM." Moses pulled on the handbrake. "You've been out for it for a couple hours."

Herron was grateful for the rest. His time in the special forces had taught him to grab sleep when he could. "Where are we?"

She shrugged. "Some patch of countryside outside of D.C. Don't ask me to point to it on a map."

Herron popped open the car door, climbed out and inhaled a lungful of cool night air. They were alone under the stars. After the ambush, they'd swapped cars twice and then made their way out of the city, stopping only to purchase food at a gas station. Moses still had her submachine gun and he had the shotgun, but they were unlikely to need the weapons here. They'd seen no further sign of any attackers and until they returned to civilization, they were probably in little danger – the Enclave team would've committed everything they had available to pull off the raid.

He sat on the ground and watched Moses exit the vehicle, illuminated by the pale light of the moon. She sat beside him, putting the submachine gun down in front of her and the plastic bag full of food and bottled water between them. It was mostly junk – she'd insisted on large amounts of chocolate – but sugar and carbs would suit him right now.

"Who was the man you lost back at the warehouse?" Herron looked at her. "I was surprised they sent in such a large team."

"His name was Gary..." Her voice trailed off for a second. "The Enclave doesn't just use single assassins. They have other resources, including tactical teams. They're enormously powerful and they'll never stop hunting you."

He almost laughed. Her remarks were a further attempt to dissuade him from getting the resources he needed and then going into hiding with Kearns. But she did have a point. After Herron's run-in with Shade at the shopping mall and the ease with which the assassin had bested him, running and hiding seemed almost futile.

They sat in silence for a few minutes, then Herron dug into the bag and pulled out a bag of Doritos. He tore them open. "So, what're you planning now? More recruiting?"

"There's nobody else to recruit. You're the last person on my list." Moses' voice was somber as she reached into the bag. "Now we fight back."

Her words surprised him – if what she'd said about the strength of the Enclave was true, Moses and her people would surely need more preparation before they were ready to strike – but her aggression was impressive. He liked that, although if Moses and her people were to win, they'd need one hell of a plan.

"How many of you are there?" Herron reached for a handful of Doritos. "If you're recruiting assassins who've turned rogue, I can't imagine there's many."

"The five of us at the warehouse, minus Gary, and one more you haven't met." She shrugged. "Numbers don't matter if we hit them hard enough."

Herron didn't necessarily agree. That sounded like a recipe to end up dead. "What'd they do to make you and your people want to fight back so hard?"

She was silent for long seconds, then she sighed. "We all have our own stories and our own reasons. I was sent to Mexico and tasked with blowing up a warehouse full of drugs. I infiltrated, killed the sentries, set the explosives and bugged out. After it exploded, I watched it burn and heard the screams. There were dozens of people in there."

"Who were they?"

She stared off into the distance. "Illegal immigrants preparing to cross the border into the United States. The warehouse was full of drugs, sure. I saw them. What I didn't see was the holding pens full of desperate people who'd paid the cartel to get them over the border. I confronted my handler about it and got nothing but silence. That's when I knew it'd been deliberate, not telling me about them first."

Herron couldn't see why she'd lie about what had happened – and so pick a fight with such terrible odds of survival – but he also couldn't see who'd benefit from killing a bunch of refugees. The U.S. Government? He'd always assumed the jobs his handler assigned him were conducted with official federal sanction. "Who ordered the mission?"

"Who knows? Some of our jobs were for the Government, but others could've been for different employers. All I know is the Enclave is morally bankrupt. From my own experience and listening to the others, it's clear to me that for all the good they do, there's just as much evil – it's all about the profit."

"So you started a war."

"I couldn't live with what I've done otherwise. I've learned their agenda and their secrets and found enough allies to fight back." She looked at him. "Allies like you."

Herron shook his head. To the best of his knowledge, he'd only ever killed those who deserved it, but in targeting Kearns and killing Christopher the Enclave had shown they'd target innocents too. Was that enough to join Moses' moral crusade? "There's a woman I promised to keep safe. I met you to see if you'd be able to help me do that, but what you're asking just puts us both in more danger."

"It does. But if we don't do this, you'll spend forever looking over your shoulder for the next Enclave assassin to find you. If we pull it off, you'll both be safe forever."

"This war... more innocents will die."

"And if we do nothing, the Enclave will keep killing the guilty and innocent depending on who's paying. We need to stop it, even if there's a cost."

There was a long pause. Herron needed to know if he could trust her before he could decide anything. He changed the topic to test that trust in a small way. "What's your name?"

"You don't like Moses? I thought it was kind of smart, given I was leading you to safety." She pushed herself to her feet. "It's Jessica. Now, are you sticking around?"

Herron nodded and stood up. "For now."

\* \* \*

Herron and Jessica arrived safely in Washington D.C.

a few hours later, just as the sun was peeking over the horizon and the morning traffic was building on the highways into the city. They avoided the procession downtown. Instead, Jessica pulled up in the parking lot of an old, dank-looking motel, the sort of place that might charge by the hour.

Jessica killed the engine and smiled. "Here we are, then. Paradise. Leave the guns."

Herron hesitated. They'd stowed their weapons in the trunk, not wanting a passing cop to spot their hardware, and he'd been fine with that. But being unarmed now made him uneasy. While he trusted this woman a little, he'd trust her a hell of a lot more with a 12-gauge in his hands, at least until she told him her plan.

She wasn't waiting for him to argue, though, and by the time he was out of the car she was halfway to the motel reception. Herron followed, taking the time to look around. The other cars in the parking lot were all newer European models, the sign out front flashed 'NO VACANCY' and the blinds were drawn in every window. He didn't sense any immediate threat, but something didn't sit quite right either. The motel felt unwelcoming, as if someone had gone out of their way to make it so.

The reception area was empty and Jessica slipped around the front desk and into the back room, Herron a couple of steps behind her.

Three men sat on sofas around a coffee table, on

which lay an arsenal of weapons and a laptop. Herron recognized them all as having survived the ambush at the warehouse.

"You know Ben..." Jessica sat heavily on one of the sofas.

"Sure. The loudmouth," Herron replied, earning himself a glare.

Jessica laughed. "And that's Kellen and Greg."

Herron nodded at them, his gaze settling on the laptop screen as he did so. It was showing a loop of security-camera feeds. Suddenly, everything made complete sense. "You guys rented the whole motel?"

"Why not?" Ben gave a short laugh. "We found all this money just sitting on the seat of a car in Baltimore."

Herron wasn't amused. That money had been his ticket out. "I hope whatever is left will find its way back to me."

"Think of it as security bond for good behavior." Ben's smirk widened and Herron considered punching it off his face.

"That's enough." Jessica gestured for Herron to sit. "Herron still isn't sure whether he's in or he's out, but I think I made a compelling case."

"You mightn't need to." Greg's face darkened. "We heard from Ella an hour ago. There's been an incident."

The mood in the room soured. Still standing, Herron looked at each of them and crossed his arms, waiting for someone to fill him in. "Who's Ella?"

"One of us." Jessica's expression was grim. "I put her on a special assignment right after we sprang you from the shopping mall."

No matter how bad he was at interpersonal communication and emotional intelligence, Herron didn't like where this was going. "What sort of special assignment?"

"Ella was tracking you to make sure you arrived at the meeting in Baltimore. We didn't want you to fall victim to the Enclave." Jessica shrugged. "But when we realized you had a friend who was also an Enclave target and that you were leaving her behind, I told Ella to stay in Maryland to keep an eye on her."

Herron's eyes narrowed. "Why would you need to do that?"

"To keep her safe..." She regarded him, her eyes shifty. "Or to use as leverage if you didn't agree to join us."

Greg cleared his throat. "The Enclave sent an operative to take out your friend, but she's safe. Ella is watching over her and will continue to keep her that way."

Herron ground his teeth. Jessica had played him by tasking an asset to sit on Kearns. This Ella had kept Kearns safe from another Enclave attack, but she also acted as a blade, hanging above Kearns' head.

And above his. "So, you decided that your best method of recruiting me was to blackmail me?"

Anger flashed across Jessica's face. "I want you to join us voluntarily, but failing that I'm happy to use your friend to get you on our side. The Enclave isn't just going after us. Our friends and family are in danger, too. We're desperate and, to me, the ends totally justify the means. There's no neutrality in this war. You're with us or you're against us."

"So, what happens if I decide to hit the road?"

"You know who we are and what we're doing. You wouldn't make it out of this room." Her eyes were cold, serious – Herron didn't doubt she'd make good on the threat. "The Enclave is trying to kill you and your friend. I'm asking you to help us save you both. With us, there's a choice: you're in or you're dead. With them, you're just dead."

"You think you could take me down that easily?"

"Put your dick away before it gets you into trouble." The man Jessica had identified as Kellen fixed Herron with a hard stare. "She's an Alpha, buddy. She could take any of us down without breaking a sweat."

"What the fuck is an Alpha?"

"The Enclave's primary operatives. There's only two of them."

Jessica held up a hand, interrupting her man. "What he's trying to say is that my dick is bigger than all of yours. Now, can we get back to focusing on what matters? I've saved your ass twice, Mitch. Now I need you. Help me and I'll keep your friend safe."

Herron let out a sigh. She had a point. At worst, he had no choice. At best, he now knew someone was looking out for Kearns. "So what's the plan? Hanging out in motels?"

Jessica's face stayed serious, his joke falling flat. "Oh, we have bigger plans than this, Mitch. I think you're going to like what we have in store. You might even thank me for forcing you along for the ride. It'll even prove to you that I'm not lying about the Enclave targeting innocents. We're going to stop them."

Herron finally took a seat on the sofa. "I'm listening."

"That's not even the best part." She smiled. "The Enclave's other Alpha is a friend of yours. And we're going to take him down."

\* \* \*

Herron massaged his temples. It felt like they'd been talking for hours. "If Alphas are gods and Shade is an Alpha, how am I still alive?"

"You got lucky," Jessica answered. "He was kicking your ass. Even with our help it was a close call. The thing about Alphas is we don't fail. I suspect you were his first."

Herron nodded. He didn't think she was

embellishing the potency of the Alphas. Only instinct had got him off the bus and Shade had nearly succeeded in ending him at the mall. If there was a third encounter, Herron wasn't sure he'd survive. That didn't mean he wouldn't kill for another chance to take Shade down, though.

Jessica and her team had told him all he wanted to know about the Enclave and their campaign against it, and more besides... all he needed was proof of the organization targeting innocents.

"Don't worry." Kellen seemed to mistake Herron's silence for concern. "We can take him down. Bullets, explosives, blades, a motor-vehicle collision..."

"Stick to the plan." Jessica's voice cut him short. "We've already lost Gary and a hard task is now a hell of a lot harder. But we can do it."

"We're invisible to them now until we strike," Greg put his feet up on the coffee table. "Whereas they still have clients to satisfy and targets to take out. We're going to exploit that to save an innocent, capture Shade and use him to find a handler. Once we've got a handler, we can blow the doors open on their whole operation. It's a good plan."

Jessica nodded and ran him through the plan. It was simple, but also bold, aggressive and violent – exactly the sort of move a small group of partisans needed to strike at a superior foe – and by the time Jessica had finished talking, any doubt Herron had about siding with her and her crew had been overtaken by his desire to get another shot at Shade.

Herron had one more question. He'd seen harebrained schemes succeed simply through superior firepower, and simple jobs fail through lack of it. "What gear do we have?"

"We've managed to cobble together some odds and ends. Come take a look." Jessica stood and led Herron and the team back out to the motel reception – behind the desk, out of sight of the door, were two large duffel bags near the wall. She gestured at them, like a gameshow host revealing a prize. "Go ahead."

Herron unzipped one of the bags and smiled. Inside were pistols, assault rifles and everything in between. He could also see grenades, knives, silencers, scopes, tactical vests and all the spare ammunition they could ever want. It mightn't be enough to take down an army, but Herron was confident it'd give them a reasonable chance.

"Okay." Herron laughed and turned to Jessica. "Your cock is definitely bigger than mine. No contest."

"We're not amateurs. We've been planning this for a while and we don't intend to screw it up. It's all locked and loaded and ready to go."

Herron inspected a few of the guns. All were top quality. It wasn't the sort of arsenal you could just whip up. He inspected a pistol. "You might just pull this off."

"*We* might just pull this off." Ben stepped closer and got into Herron's face. "*We* lost one of our own back at the warehouse trying to get you out. *You* better be worth it. Or else."

In one swift movement, Herron snatched up a pistol and swung it in an arc at Ben's head. It connected with a sickening crack somewhere near his temple.

As Ben staggered back, his hands up to shield his head from further blows, Herron kicked straight at his stomach. Ben gasped, and Herron flicked off the pistol's safety, pointed it at him. Jessica hadn't moved an inch. Neither had the rest of the team. They seemed content to let Herron and Ben sort this one out. That was fine with Herron.

"Get something straight." Herron's voice was ice-cold. "I'm here because I choose to be. Don't threaten me again."

Ben glared with hate-filled eyes. "You better hope Jessica stays on her feet, because the second she's no longer the boss, you're a dead man."

Herron pulled the trigger.

He'd placed the shot wide, but not by much. Ben's hand flew to his ear, blood oozing between his fingers.

Herron raised an eyebrow. "Clear?"

Ben's gaze went to the floor. "Clear."

"Good. Herron tossed the pistol back into the trunk.

Herron walked out into the night. He'd made his decision. Now that he was sure they had the gear to pull off the plan, he was along for the ride. First came sleep, though. There was no use having exclusive use of a motel if he couldn't catch some shut-eye. He had no idea what to expect tomorrow, when the hunt for Shade began, but he'd face it fresh and rested.

And with both ears intact.

## 7

HERRON WOKE WITH A START, blinking and struggling to focus. His nightmares had made their usual visit and a moment ago he'd been firing endless pistol rounds into the shambling corpse of a target he'd killed a decade ago. But at least he'd clocked some rest – if he was going to be charging at the most capable killer on Earth, he'd prefer not to do it yawning.

Fifteen minutes later, he was showered and ready to go. He had nothing to pack, so he simply walked out into the daylight, closing the door behind him. He'd shut his eyes and was enjoying the warmth of the sun on his face when a footstep crunched on the gravel beside him.

Herron opened his eyes and saw Jessica holding a cardboard carry tray with two takeout cups in it. Herron took one. "Thanks."

She leaned against the brick wall. "Sleep well?"

"You tell me. You were watching my room all night."

Jessica nodded. "We're watching the whole motel and everything within five blocks."

"No sign of the Enclave?" Herron sipped his coffee. "I half expected to wake up to Shade smiling down at me."

"Then I doubt you'd have woken up at all. We'd have seen him, but we wouldn't have been able to help you in time."

She turned and led him to the parked cars. The other members of Jessica's crew were spilling out of the motel office and into the parking lot, like they'd been up and ready for hours. Herron wasn't surprised to have been left out of the early-morning conversations. He was new on the scene. They didn't know him, so Jessica was controlling the information he received. He'd have done the same thing if he were in her shoes.

It didn't matter. He knew his role: Help to kill Shade.

Kellen opened the trunk of his car, revealing the arsenal still in the duffel bags. Herron rifled through the guns and selected a silenced pistol. It was a relatively modest weapon compared to the heavy firepower on offer, but it suited his role in the plan. He stuffed it into the waistband of his jeans.

"You sure you wouldn't prefer something with a bit more grunt?" Kellen held up a submachine gun.

Herron filled his pockets with a few spare magazines. "This suits me fine. If you guys do your job, I won't need it."

Ben had a weapon in each hand and was tapping them against his legs in some out-of-time tune. "Good to go?"

"Last thing." Jessica produced a bag the size of a glasses case and unzipped it. "I want everyone in touch throughout the whole operation."

She held out an earpiece to Herron. It was state-of-the-art gear, with a built-in microphone – he'd be able to hear the whole team and would only need to speak very softly to be heard in return. He twisted it into his ear and waited while the others did the same. Then, as soon as everyone had tested the technology, the team split up and headed to their assigned vehicles.

Jessica and Ben took one car, Kellen and Greg another, leaving Herron to ride solo in the SUV he'd arrived in. Jessica had left the keys in the ignition for him and in an instant the SUV's engine roared to life. As he disengaged the handbrake, he didn't even glance at Jessica and her team, just shifted the car into gear and floored it.

\* \* \*

"I'm five minutes out." Herron looked down at the SUV's navigation screen. "Everything good to go?"

"*Okay.*" Jessica's voice was loud and clear in his ear. "*We're all in place, Mitch.*"

The hotel was just up ahead. The others had trickled in over the last hour and Herron would be the last to arrive, allowing everyone else to get in position. As he covered the final mile to his destination, he ran through the plan again in his head. Jessica had let him in on the detail only at the very last minute, when all the pieces were in place.

While Jessica was limited in the number of field operatives she had at her disposal, they weren't her only assets. It appeared not everyone in the Enclave was willing to take up arms, there were those inside the organization who were willing to fight in other ways – with information. It was from one of these leaks that Jessica had learned about David Hogan.

The CEO of a Fortune 500 company, Hogan was the kind of corporate fat cat that made up in body weight and wealth what he lacked in hair and charm. But while Herron found such men personally distasteful, Hogan had done nothing wrong in the pursuit of his business. Nothing except upset the Enclave's interests, at least. The way Jessica's mole told it, Shade had been tasked to take Hogan down as soon as Herron was dealt with – but with Herron inconveniently failing to die, and the businessman only in town for a day, Shade would have to make his move on Hogan now.

Their plan was simple: keep Hogan covered until Shade appeared and then capture the enemy Alpha.

The deadliest man on Earth was close and Herron was headed straight for him. For the first time in his life, Herron felt nervous about a mission. He was no slouch in the business of death, but Shade...

...Shade might actually kill him.

Herron pulled into the hotel parking area, switched off the engine and got out. A valet rushed over to him. Herron tossed the keys to the man. "Here you go, pal."

The valet smiled wide. "Hello, sir. Do you have a reservation?"

"Dave Hogan." His first part in the plan was to make sure the doomed entrepreneur had checked in.

The valet nodded, punched something into his iPad and then frowned. "Sir, it says Mr Hogan has already checked in and parked his vehicle."

"He's my lover." He dug into his pocket and produced some cash. "Could you take care of the car please?"

"Of course, sir. We've got some spaces free." The valet winked at Herron, took the cash and headed for the SUV.

Herron entered the lobby and headed straight for the check-in counter. Kellen was standing at the concierge desk, flicking through brochures, but

Herron couldn't see the rest of Jessica's team. He knew they'd be close.

At the counter, an army of good-looking young staff members waited with smiles on their faces. If they knew the violence that was about to be inflicted inside their hotel, Herron doubted they'd be so cheery.

"May I help you, sir?" A young blonde staffer asked.

"Could you check if Mr Hogan is in his room?"

"Of course." She reached for a phone and dialed. "One moment."

"Thanks."

The receptionist frowned and put the phone down. "Mr Hogan has his telephone set to the do not disturb setting. I can't get through, but he hasn't left his key with us, so that'd suggest he's in. If you like, I—"

Herron held up a hand. "He's probably asleep. We had a late night. I'll catch up with him later."

He left her to it and headed for a cluster of expensive leather sofas that ringed a hardwood coffee table. He sat facing the bank of elevators, reached behind his back and pulled out his pistol, which he kept in his hand covered with a cushion. Now it was a waiting game. They had no doubt Shade would come for Hogan: when an Enclave operative was assigned a target, they completed the mission or died trying.

Herron was counting on that.

"I'm in position." He spoke softly, knowing the high-quality comms gear would pick up his voice. "Reception just confirmed Hogan is in his room."

"*Excellent.*" Jessica's voice had a nervous edge. "*Greg and I will breach his room, secure him and wait for Shade to arrive. You guys stay in the lobby. Remember, we need Shade alive.*"

As he settled back for confirmation that Jessica had completed her task, Herron kept his eyes locked on the elevator bay, knowing the others were watching the stairwells. His mind worked overtime, probing Jessica's plan for any weaknesses that could allow Shade to escape, but he came up blank. The plan was good. Once they had Hogan under guard, the trap would be set. if Shade somehow made it out, Herron and the others would be ready to hit him in the lobby.

Jessica radioed situation reports. "*We've reached the door... Scanning cloned access pass... Breaching.*"

Herron held his breath. Seconds passed with no update and he started to lose patience. "Anything?"

"*No. There's luggage and the bed has been used, but there's nobody here. Could he have gone out and not left his key at reception?*"

"Something feels wrong." Herron tensed. "We need to abort."

"*Not a chance.*" Ben's voice now. "*Like Jessica said, he's probably just stepped out for a minute. We can't surrender this advantage. We can still get Shade.*"

Herron knew it was a mistake to stay. Their business required detachment and the ability to know when to pull back and try again later. Herron's instincts nagged at him to do just that – withdraw, regroup – but that'd mean leaving Jessica and her team potentially high and dry. He focused on his role in the plan, monitored the elevator, wondering how much longer Jessica would have them sit here exposed.

Seconds ticked by. Every time one of the elevator doors opened Herron was ready to start shooting, but nobody emerged except businessmen and holidaymakers. There was no sign of the scarred menace who'd almost killed him at the shopping mall.

He tried again. "Our intel is wrong, Jessica. We should bug out and reassess."

"*Shut your mouth, pal.*" Ben's voice came over the communications network, but he was also close enough for Herron to hear him in person. "*You're not top dog here.*"

"*Ease up on that, Ben.*" Jessica's tone had changed. There was doubt in her voice now. "*Herron's right, we're bugging out. I—*"

Her voice was lost as somewhere, high above the lobby, an explosion boomed.

* * *

"Fuck!" Herron tore his earpiece out as the sound of the explosion tortured his ear.

As the sound of the detonation faded, he scanned the lobby. The place was awash with activity. Staff and guests were either running away or standing shell-shocked, their screams competing with the blaring of the fire alarms. Herron's gaze slipped over them, located Kellen and Ben. Both were staring at him and the implication was clear: the plan had gone wrong and Herron was the newest member of the team...

He didn't blame them – he'd be thinking exactly the same thing. But he knew what they didn't – that he hadn't been the one to screw up. He replaced his earpiece. "I'm heading up. You guys wait here and watch for Shade."

Without waiting for confirmation, he headed to the stairs. The plan had gone shit, which meant Shade must've known they were coming and turned the tables on Jessica and her crew. It sounded like Hogan's room had been rigged to blow, but Herron wouldn't know for sure until he got there to help Jessica and Greg.

If there was anything left to help.

He reached the stairs and panicked guests were pouring out. Herron tried to fight past them, but the mass of humanity was impenetrable. Though taking the elevator in this situation was a stupid idea, he needed to get upstairs *fast*. He gave up on the stairs and headed for an elevator. He pressed the button for Hogan's floor and the doors closed. The second he was alone, he drew his pistol from behind his back.

He didn't know what he was going to find up there, but he'd be ready for it.

The elevator made it five floors before there was another explosion. This one was more muffled – more distant – and didn't blast Herron's ear in the same way as the earlier detonation. It had to have come from somewhere more distant, away from Jessica and Greg's microphones. A second later the elevator stopped moving and the main lights went out.

Herron sighed and mashed the buttons on the console as pale orange emergency lighting came on. It was no good. He was trapped.

He couldn't wait for the elevator to get moving again or for someone to pry him out. Above him, he spotted a locked panel that'd give him access to the shaft. Putting the pistol back in the waistband of his jeans with one hand, he took his bump keys from his pocket with the other.

He placed his hands on the walls of the elevator car and his left foot on the safety rail, then pushed up to stand fully on the rail. Keeping one hand on the wall to steady himself, he reached for the panel with the bump keys. It was a stretch and his movements were awkward, but in a few moments he'd unlocked it and pushed it open.

Herron gripped the rim of the access hatch and pulled himself up into the darkened shaft. The only light was from the elevator he'd just escaped and the emergency lighting bleeding in between the cracks of doors above.

A maintenance ladder was built into the side of the shaft, and he seized a rung and started to climb. He made it a half-dozen floors when the light below him grew brighter. The lights inside the elevator were back on. A second later there was a whirring sound and the empty car began to rise – fast. Herron cursed and climbed more quickly, his muscles straining from the exertion.

By the time he reached the next set of doors in the shaft, he had only seconds to act.

He forced them open and crawled out, collapsing on the carpet as the elevator whizzed past him. Water rained down on him, and after a moment to catch his breath, he looked up. The fire-suppression system had activated and sprinklers were dousing the entire corridor. More by luck than judgment, he realized, he'd pulled himself out on Hogan's floor, and the scene that greeted him was carnage.

He was alone – any guests and staff must've long since fled the scene. Down the hall, the door to Hogan's room was blown open. Flash burns and the sprinklers had turned the immediate vicinity into a blackened, soaking mess. Greg's body lay right outside the room, utterly still and crumpled in an unnatural pose. The force of the explosion must've thrown him out of the door and into the wall.

Herron climbed to his feet and drew his pistol. There was no sign of Hogan or Jessica. They might be vapor, but he had to try find to them.

He moved along the doorway, pistol scanning for a target – for Shade – as he approached the room. He paused to relieve Greg of his submachine gun, looping the sling over his shoulder, then slipped inside.

The room was heavily damaged, windows were blown out and furniture turned to kindling, but the sprinklers had put out any flames. Herron cleared the bedroom and living area, then moved into the bathroom. He lowered his pistol at the sight of Jessica sitting on the tiled floor with her back to the bathtub. Her head was slumped forward, with her chin on her chest.

Herron slid onto his knees beside her and checked for a pulse. She was alive! Somehow, she'd survived the bomb and had no visible injuries.

Keeping both his pistol and his eyes on the bathroom door, he grabbed a fistful of material near Jessica's neck and shook her. He needed to get her back to her feet quickly, before the cops and hotel security arrived. Worse, Shade might show up to deal with anyone who'd survived the explosion.

Their plan had been a terrible failure but now he had to focus on survival.

After a few moments, Jessica coughed and opened her eyes. She blinked, confused, then quickly got her bearings. "I feel like I've gone three rounds with a pickup truck."

"It was a setup. Shade knew we were coming." Herron held out a hand to help her up. "He might have more surprises in store. We need to get out of here."

She took his hand and keyed her mike as she climbed off the floor. "It's Jessica. Head to the parking garage and we'll bug out."

"*Okay, Jessica.*" Ben paused. "*Greg?*"

Jessica looked at Herron. When he shook his head, she sighed. "Greg didn't make it, guys."

Herron followed her out into the corridor. Jessica paused for a second when she saw Greg's body and then they were moving again, taking the stairs down to the basement parking garage. He wasn't sure about the plan, but she was in charge and he'd follow her.

When at last they burst out of the stairwell and into the gloomy carpark, however, his ill-feelings were justified. At the far end of the garage, a shadowy figure waited behind a car, an assault rifle propped on its hood and leveled at Herron and Jessica.

Shade grinned and opened fire.

---

## 8

"DOWN!"

Herron barged Jessica with his hip, knocking her to the ground. He dived after her, landing hard as rounds pounded into the concrete wall behind him, and scrambled to cover behind a Toyota sedan. He and Jessica sheltered behind its hood, keeping the engine block between them and Shade as the Alpha's fire perforated the bodywork. Whoever owned the car was going to have one hell of an insurance claim.

"Close but no cigar!" Shade's shout dripped with mockery. "There's two of you and one of me, though. I hoped it'd be a fair fight!"

Herron gripped Greg's submachine gun tight and glanced at Jessica. She didn't look wounded. "You okay?"

"I'm fine!" Jessica had to raise her voice as more

shots slammed into the sedan. "How'd he know we'd be here?"

Herron had his suspicions. "We can figure that out later."

Jessica nodded then peered around the car, only for the ferocity of the gunfire to increase. "We're pinned."

The clatter of the assault rifle died was replaced by Shade's shout. "If you guys want to have some fun, we better hurry up! The cops will be on their way!"

Herron gritted his teeth and looked around, searching for an edge. Shade had them boxed in, but two-to-one odds had to count for something. "Wait here and fire at him every ten seconds. Make sure you're on time."

Something flickered across Jessica's face – clearly she wasn't used to being ordered around – then she nodded. She popped from cover and fired, the reports booming in the echoing space.

Herron broke cover and sprinted, betting everything on the hope that Shade would duck when he was being fired on. He made it to the next car without being pierced by hot lead, counted down ten seconds and then moved again as Jessica opened fire. After three more bursts her magazine was empty and Herron was closer to having the drop on Shade, but he was still not close enough. The Alpha was at the far end of the garage and had a sightline on all except the far-most cars on either side of him. Herron wanted to get 90 degrees side-on to Shade, taking his cover out of the equation so he could force him to surrender.

Herron was glad Jessica had the sense to switch out her magazine and keep to schedule, firing another short burst. Herron scrambled, moving from car to car in time with Jessica's diversions, expecting with every step to catch a bullet. Sooner or later Shade would figure out what was going on, but Herron had to hope he was in position before that happened.

And then he had a clear line on the target. He crouched low behind a BMW, steadied his submachine gun on the trunk and took aim at Shade. All thoughts of capturing the enemy Alpha were now gone. He was going to terminate his ass.

Ben's stupidity was the only thing that stopped Herron from capturing Shade. Kellen threw the door to the garage open and both he and Ben stormed through it. As soon as he saw Shade, Ben dived for cover and shouted a warning for everyone to stay down. Kellen wasn't quite so smart. He pulled up short and stared at Shade, clearly not expecting to see him there.

Shade fired a quick burst at Kellen and then ducked. Herron lost sight of his target and he looked around frantically to reacquire his target. After five seconds of searching, a steel door slammed and Herron knew Shade had escaped, retreating when the odds against him became too great.

All their work had been for nothing.

Herron stormed across the parking garage and aimed his submachine gun at Ben's head. Immediately, both Jessica and Kellen aimed their weapons at Herron. It was a standoff between four of the deadliest operatives on the planet.

"You prick!" Ben shouted. "What're you doing?"

"The only way Shade could know we were coming is if someone sold us out. If *you* sold us out." His eyes were locked on Ben, his index finger was half squeezed back on the trigger. He'd suspected Ben was dirty and the way his shouted warning had given Shade a chance to escape all but confirmed it.

Herron snarled at Ben. "It can't have been me – I didn't know the safe house location when The Enclave raided it. They might've figured that out by following us from the meeting, but then they blew up a plan I didn't know any details about until the last minute. That says we have a mole. Jessica was in Hogan's room when the bomb went off and Greg died in the blast, which rules them out. That leaves two possible options: You or Kellen."

"Fucking hell." Jessica shifted her aim to Kellen. "Which one of you pricks was it?"

Ben's eyes were wide. "Why do you think it was me?"

Herron laughed. "You've been rattling my cage

since I joined the team. You were at the safe house. You tried to stop me from being recruited. You didn't want to abort just prior to the bombs going off. You shouted a warning just as I was about to capture Shade, like we originally intended..."

Jessica cut in. "But when Shade fired on Kellen he missed. For a normal operative, that'd be strange. For an Alpha, it's impossible."

"Shit." Ben shook his head. "When we were in the lobby, Kellen turned off his comms and told me we should bug out through the entrance. He delayed us getting down here."

Kellen sighed and flashed a humorless smile at Jessica. "Your little rebellion is over. The Enclave knew what you were doing every step of the way. I—"

Herron shifted his aim and fired a burst into Kellen's head. "152."

\* \* \*

"So what now?"

Herron sat on a sofa opposite Jessica and Ben. They'd managed to escape the hotel, evade the cops, swap out their vehicles and make it to a motel in a town somewhere outside Washington D.C. They didn't know what had become of Hogan – if the CEO had even been at the hotel at all. Either Jessica's mole had been wrong or Kellen had sold them out to Shade and the Enclave. It didn't matter. The mole was burned and Jessica's team had lost three people in as many days.

They needed a next move. If there *was* a next move.

A knock at the door shattered the silence. Herron sidled up to the peephole and peered through: it was the Dominos delivery driver. He opened the door and made small talk with the driver as he swapped three large pizzas for a twenty-dollar bill. In less than 30 seconds, the driver was gone and Herron was depositing the pizzas on the coffee table. He devoured the first slice before noticing neither Jessica nor Ben was eating. He'd hoped the food would break the impasse, but they were acting like sullen children.

Herron finished his pizza and stared at them. "Enough sulking, both of you. I asked what now."

Ben grimaced. "Without capturing Shade and then a handler, we can't execute the next phase of our plan. That was our only shot."

Herron frowned. "Can't we get our hands on one another way?"

"It's not that easy. Not now we know our mole inside the Enclave must be bullshit too." Ben shrugged and reached for a slice. On the trip to the motel the trio had discussed the situation a little and realized that since the mole was Kellen's asset, almost every piece of intel they'd received from him had to be tainted. Ben had clearly given up. "They don't know where we are and we don't know where they are. We're blind."

"Plus they have more of every other resource than we do." Jessica spoke her first words in almost half an hour. "We've lost everything. It's over."

Herron sneered. Jessica had convinced him to try to take down the Enclave, now she was giving up? "I thought you guys had more guts than this."

Jessica's eyes narrowed. "I had plenty of guts when I saved your ass those few times."

"So what happened to them?"

Herron got up and headed for the bedroom. He wanted to grab some sleep before hitting the road tomorrow, even though it was still the middle of the afternoon. If Jessica didn't want to fight, he wouldn't try to convince her. He'd go back to his old plan: disappear with Kearns. Though the Enclave and Shade would still be on his tail, it seemed a better idea than sticking with a group that'd given up the fight.

He closed the door, stripped down to his underwear and climbed into bed. The mattress was hard and uncomfortable, but it suited him fine. There were a hundred worse places he'd bedded down for the night. He put his pistol on the side table, closed his eyes and drifted off.

His victims came for him in his sleep, like they always did, and it seemed like only moments before he woke again drenched in sweat. He rubbed his face and looked around. He didn't know what time it was, but the afternoon sunlight that had been peeking in through the curtains when he got his head down had been replaced by the darkness of night.

He closed his eyes and was almost asleep again when the floor creaked. He opened his eyes and reached for his pistol, but a firm hand grabbed his wrist. Jessica was standing over him, the connecting door to her room ajar. There was enough light that he could see the resolve on her face, but there was also a softness in her features that surprised him.

She released his wrist. "I wanted to apologize for using your friend to blackmail you. That was wrong. And I understand if you want to leave."

Herron considered his next words carefully. "I agreed to help you take down Shade and the Enclave. We're not done yet."

"You'll stick with us?"

"Sure. If you keep fighting." He paused. "Put the setback behind you, forget about things for tonight, get back up tomorrow and keep leading."

"Some army I've got, huh?" She gave a bitter laugh. "All right. Tomorrow we figure out what comes next and how to take the fight to them again."

"Okay." Herron regarded her quizzically. "What're you do—"

She held her index finger up to her lips to silence him, then unbuttoned and removed her black blouse.

Her cream-colored bra was off next, revealing breasts that were small and shapely.

"You suggested we forget about things for the night. This seems like a good way to do that." Then she paused. She had a sly look in her eyes. "Just sex. Nothing more. Okay?"

Herron nodded. He was fine with a little recreation.

She unbuttoned her pants and let them fall to the floor. Like her bra, her underwear was functional and the furthest thing from lingerie-store sexy that he could imagine, but that only made her even more appealing. Within seconds, she was naked at the foot of the bed.

"Well?" She put a hand on her hip and raised an eyebrow. "What the hell are you waiting for?"

"The end of the preview." Herron threw the covers off. "We're not going to both fit in this bed."

She glanced down at his underwear. "We'll just have to do some rearranging, put some things inside others and make it work."

They made it work.

\* \* \*

"That was... energetic." Jessica snuggled in to him tightly, breathing heavily

Herron grunted. She was right. It had been a constant struggle for dominance. They were both strong and athletic, a fact that had led to a range of pleasing outcomes. She'd finished first, but had been generous in helping him over the line. It wasn't the best sex he'd ever had, but it was the best he'd had in a while.

Her fingers traced along his body, locating his scars. He explained them all: the deep stab wound in his thigh, the gunshot wound in his shoulder, countless others. He'd earned them all in the Special Forces or, later, working as a contractor for the Enclave. He found no such scars on her body, which suggested she was better at the job. She *was* an Alpha.

Once their breathing was back to normal, Herron maneuvered his body so he could look at her. "What now?"

Jessica sighed. "We wanted to capture a handler because there's a gathering of the Enclave's leadership next week. I know that for a fact, because before I went rogue they were talking to me about using the Alphas – me and Shade – to defend it. If we can get a handler, we can find out where it's happening."

Herron's eyes narrowed. "So any handler could lead you to the rest of the leadership."

"In theory. They'll all be attending. We only need one."

While Herron considered this, they settled into comfortable silence. Before long, Jessica was asleep.

As he lay there enjoying the warmth of her naked body pressed into his and the quiet sound of her breathing, he planned. He knew he needed to take the fight into his own hands and the information about the leadership gathering might just give him what he needed to do it.

A few hours passed before he'd figured it out in his head. His move was going to be less complex, less aggressive than taking down Shade and using him to capture a handler.

Carefully he uncoupled himself from Jessica and climbed out of bed. She sucked in a breath, grumbled in protest and rolled over. He paused until her breathing confirmed she was sound asleep, then dressed in the dark. She didn't move again, not even when he grabbed his pistol and hit the same creaking floorboard she'd trodden on when coming to his bed.

When he was clear of the room, he moved quietly across the living room, where weapons and ammunition were scattered around the pizza boxes. Ben was sleeping soundly on the sofa, with his submachine gun for a bedfellow. Perhaps they shouldn't have skimped on renting a third room after all. Herron started past him and then did a double take.

Two of the three pizzas he'd ordered were untouched.

He scoffed two slices of cold pizza, then walked to the kitchenette and grabbed a bottle of water. The sex had been energetic and sweaty, so he needed to refuel and hydrate. Before heading for the front door, he grabbed one of the pizza boxes. It'd keep him going on the road.

Standing alone in the parking lot, he sucked in a deep breath of cool night air. He was looking forward to getting on the road again, though he didn't think Jessica would be thrilled when she realized he was gone. Her reaction would be something to behold after he'd told her he'd stick with her.

He crossed the street, walking right past the car he'd arrived in and headed instead for a plain white Toyota. Using his bump keys, he broke into the Toyota and he had it started inside of a minute. He placed the pizza box on the passenger seat and hid the pistol in the glove compartment, then, keeping the headlights off until he was away from the motel, he signaled and pulled onto the road.

This time, he didn't need directions. He knew exactly where he was going.

He was driving back into his past.

## 9

HERRON'S SHIT list had a new addition after the incident at the hotel – elevators. That didn't remove the need to ride one up to the eleventh floor of this Washington D.C. apartment block. Not if he wanted to find the answers he needed to get back on the trail of the Enclave leadership, anyway.

The digital display ticked up through the floors and Herron breathed a sigh of relief when this elevator succeeded where the last one had failed. He stepped out into a softly lit hallway filled with bland artwork and ranks of identical apartment doors. He counted off the numbers on them until he came to 1114.

Standing to the side of the door so no one could see him through the peephole, Herron knocked. There was no response, so he tried again, pounding the door with his closed fist. Someone inside the apartment cursed and footsteps approached the door. As it opened, Herron stepped through and confronted the occupant.

Herron smiled. "Good to see you, Michael."

"What're *you* doing here?"

It was a fair question. Until a year ago, Herron hadn't thought about Michael Reeves in more than a decade. He'd once saved Reeves' life in Hong Kong but had never expected to call in the favor, because the Enclave had always provided all the resources he'd needed. But now he was on his own, he'd used Reeves to end the threat of the Omega Strain. Now Herron was returning to the well.

"I'm here to ask for a favor." Herron raised his pistol. "Let's go inside."

As soon as he saw the gun, Reeves' eyes widened and he backed away. Herron followed him and kicked the door closed behind them, locking them inside. Reeves' eyes darted from the pistol, to the door, to the windows. Looking for a way to escape was an entirely natural reaction, but Herron didn't have time to waste.

He injected some menace into his voice. "Whenever you're done, let's talk."

"No." Reeves' voice had a surprising amount of resolve. "You said we were square."

"Things have changed. I need something else."

Reeves sagged. He was one of the smartest men on Earth, a senior analyst at the National Security

Agency responsible for sifting through a billion specks of electronic sand and finding treasure. He was clearly also smart enough to realize the man with the gun set the terms, no matter the previous deal. He led Herron into a small dining room and sat in a chair at the table.

Herron sat opposite and placed the pistol on the wooden surface, close enough that he could reach it and Reeves couldn't. He leaned forward. "How's the spook business?"

Reeves sneered, a little more relaxed now the gun was off him. "How's the killer business?"

"A little slow lately, actually. I'm a freelancer these days."

"Really?" Reeves' surprise was plain. "Okay, what do you want?"

Herron paused; what he was about to say sounded stupid. "I need to find a handler."

"Did you lose him or something?" Reeves rolled his eyes.

Herron had known this was going to be the difficult part of the conversation. Reeves was an NSA ferret who could find anything or anyone who had the slightest electronic signature. He was hoping the resources Reeves had at his disposal would be enough to pierce the veil of secrecy surrounding the Enclave.

Herron ignored the jibe. "I don't have a name, address, phone number or identifying features."

"Then why don't you just ask me to converse with the dead?" Reeves scoffed. "I'll need some details."

"Look, when I used to call my handler, I'd recite an eight-digit code for clearance. If you can flag any calls that open with a code like that and listen in on them you'll be able to tell if the person on the other end of the line is using a voice distorter. If they are, it's a good bet they're a handler."

"I—" Reeves began, then stopped and chewed his lower lip. "That *could* work."

"Good. Find me a handler and we're even. I—" Herron paused when a frown passed over Reeves' face. "What?"

"I don't have access to the computing power I'd need to scan every phone call in America for eight-digit codes. It's too broad. I'll need more information to narrow the search."

"There's none. You'll have to get access to more processing power."

Reeves was starting to panic again, his eyes shifted to the gun. "That's impossible! I can't get that kind of access by myself, not without someone noticing. I'd have to request it, be allocated it. And there's no way I can ask for computer resources of that magnitude unless I've got evidence of..."

"What?"

"Something huge, a catastrophic threat to national security like—" Reeves faltered as he realized his mistake.

Herron nodded and stood. "All right then."

"You can't do it, it'll never—"

Herron smiled. "Never say never."

* * *

Herron gripped the chain link fence, climbed over and landed on the other side. All around him were dozens of white vans with *Joe's Rentals* stenciled on the side. He had no idea who Joe was, but he was about to become a national figure. Within 24 hours his name and his vans would be splashed all over the national news, with the authorities scrambling to piece together events that had led to another terrorist attack on American soil.

This was the first stop of several he had to make tonight. He'd spent an hour using the heavily encrypted internet at Reeves' apartment to formulate a plan big enough that Reeves' bosses wouldn't question giving him the computing power he needed to prevent it. Herron was going to stage an attack on an airport big enough for the NSA to assign Reeves all the computing power at their disposal. But instead of hunting the supposed terrorists, Reeves would use the grunt of the NSA's electronic snooping systems to track the Enclave.

Herron broke into one of the vans, climbed inside and hot wired it. The first and easiest part of his plan, it went off without a hitch. Picking up speed, he drove to the exit gate and smashed into it. The chain link gates were secured only by a padlock, which couldn't resist the force of a one-ton van. With a tortured squeal they sprang apart, releasing Herron and the van from Joe's clutches and getting him on the open road.

He kept his gloves on and the balaclava over his head as he drove down the suburban roads and onto the highway, headed south. He'd chosen Joe's Rentals because it was the closest van supplier to his next stop, a farm supplies wholesaler. The largest of its kind in the north-east, it was less than 15 minutes away in the highway traffic.

When he arrived at the wholesaler, Herron removed his balaclava and stopped the van at the security checkpoint near the gate, beyond which the facility kept multiple warehouses. He wound down the window as the guard inside looked up from his magazine, removed his feet from the desk and exited his booth.

Herron smiled at the guard as he closed in. "Evening."

"It's late. We're closed."

Herron frowned, as if this was a surprise. He rubbed his chin with one hand and gripped the door handle with the other. "But I'm due back with horse feed by dawn."

"Do we look like a 24-hour McDonalds?" The

guard shook his head and placed a hand on the side of the van. "We're closed. Beat it."

Herron pulled on the door latch and pushed with all his strength. The guard cried out as the door slammed into him, overbalancing him and knocking him to the ground. Herron climbed out, pistol drawn. Towering over the man, he lashed out with his boot, striking the guard in the head and knocking him out cold.

He took a minute to tie up the guard in the security booth, then pressed the red button to open the gate, which trundled to the side on its rails. By the time he'd put his balaclava back on, the way was clear into the gigantic farming supplies complex. He drove in, snaking his way through the facility until he reached a warehouse with a large metal roller door. He backed the van up to it. He'd done his research. This was the right spot.

Leaving the engine running, Herron got out and drew his pistol. Three guards were sprinting in his direction, batons and flashlights in their hands, the beams of light dancing around the outside of the warehouse complex. They shouted at him, but slowed when they saw the gun.

"Slow down, guys." Herron aimed at them. "Drop the gear and get those hands in the air."

None of the security men had guns of their own and they looked at each other as if figuring out whether eight bucks an hour was worth a bullet. It only took one guard to comply with his instructions before his two colleagues did the same. Soon, all three were standing with their hands in the air.

"I'm your best friend, guys." Herron walked over to them. He put bullets into two of their radios and took possession of the third. "Any other robber would've killed you."

"What do you think you're going to do, you prick?" One of the guards glared at Herron. "The cops are going to be here in 10 minutes."

"Good thing I only need nine, because you're going to help me load up my van. If you do, you live."

He explained what he needed. The guards muttered and cursed, but none of them resisted. Herron kept a safe distance and his pistol trained on the men as they opened the metal roller door that separated the van from inside of the warehouse and thousands of tons of fertilizer.

Ammonium nitrate, a key ingredient of explosives.

He waited while the guards loaded thirty large bags into the back of the van, by which time the first sirens were approaching. It was time to go.

He forced the guards back into the warehouse, pulled down the roller door and locked it. They'd be out in a few minutes, but he'd be gone in less than that. He climbed into the van and drove to the front of the depot. The van was handling sluggishly with the fertilizer in the back, but he was still able to hit the open road before the cops arrived.

When he was satisfied he was in the clear, Herron relaxed a little and grabbed the radio he'd stolen from the guard. He turned it on and pressed down on the transmit button. "Hello?"

After a long few seconds, the radio squawked and a voice replied. "*Who's this? Where's Frank?*"

"Locked in a warehouse with his buddies. The cops will spring them soon enough." Herron paused. "When they do, you'll want to tell them I stole some fertilizer. Next time they see it will be at a US airport."

Herron turned off the radio and tossed it onto the floor of the van. The lights of the depot shrank to specks in his rear-vision mirror and then he was back on the highway. He still had a lot of work to do and not much of the night left to do it in, but the hardest part was now behind him. After a few more steps, he'd be able to deliver all the computer power Reeves could ever dream of.

Then he'd get back on the trail of the Enclave.

\* \* \*

Herron wound down the window and took a ticket from the machine, raising the entrance boom gate. As the barrier rose, he screwed the piece of card into a ball and tossed it onto the floor. He wasn't planning on returning, so he didn't need it. Then he accelerated and the rental van lurched forward, hauling his cargo into the long-term car park of Dulles International Airport at twenty minutes to midnight.

He cruised the aisles, searching for a space. Though it was late and there were only a few people walking to and from cars, the garage was full to bursting with vehicles. Finally, right near the back, he found a vacant spot and lodged Joe's van in between a beat-up Chevrolet and a new model BMW.

Slipping out of the van, he took a second to stretch and let out a long yawn. It had been a long night. After leaving the farm supplies wholesaler, he'd stolen more equipment from a hardware store. Then he'd found an abandoned warehouse in which to finish his work. It'd taken some time, but when he was done he had something he was really proud of – a fake bomb that looked like a real one. Combined with the theft of the fertilizer, it was more than enough to catch the attention of the authorities.

After checking to see if anyone was watching, he opened the rear doors of the van and used a cell phone he'd stolen from a man at a gas station to take some photos. When he was happy with the shots, he locked the van and walked away. All the while, he kept his gloves on to avoid leaving prints.

Strolling towards the main airport terminal, he used the phone to text the pictures to a number he'd memorized. As soon as the phone chimed, confirming the photos had been sent, he slid it under a parked car and continued walking.

Inside the terminal, there was still no sign the jig was up. The few staff and passengers around at that time of the night went about their business, ignoring him completely. All of his effort to make the bomb and get it in place had left him famished, so he found a café, selected a muffin and soda and took them to the counter.

He smiled at the cashier. "How's your night been?"

The tired-looking teenager gave his best attempt at a smile – it was more like a grimace. "Ten minutes until I'm out of here. Six twenty, thanks pal."

"Airport prices." Herron laughed as he handed over a twenty then pocketed his change. "Have a good one."

Grabbing a booth, he sat and munched on his food, keeping his eyes on the bank of televisions against the far wall of the café. It took longer than he'd expected for the 24-hour news machine to get cranking, but after about 10 minutes CNN flashed up a news alert. He lifted the soda and downed it in one gulp as the photos he'd texted to the station's tip line appeared on the screen with the caption: *VAN BOMB AT US AIRPORT?*

That was his cue.

Herron ate the last bite of his muffin and walked

out of the café just as the staff were reacting to the news. The cashier he'd spoken to earlier was talking with a colleague, wondering aloud about the odds of the bomb being at this airport. Herron hoped that the same anxiety was rising up at the NSA, where Reeves would be sitting and waiting as the story broke.

It wouldn't be enough, though. There was one more thing left to do. He walked from the café to a bank of payphones against the far wall of the terminal, relics of an older time. He fed the change from the café into the phone, picked up the handset and dialed 911. He imagined the dispatch would be melting down with reports of vans in parking lots across the country, but this would be slightly different.

The call connected in less than 10 seconds. "911. What's your emergency?"

Herron spoke softly so nobody could overhear. "I just parked a van with a bomb."

The operator paused slightly, then her training kicked in. "Where's the bomb, sir?"

"You'll need to figure it out." Herron laughed for effect. "I'll give you a clue. Are you listening?"

"Yes, sir."

"One. Seven. Nine. Eight. Four. Four. Three. One."

Herron hung up the phone. He turned and left the bank of payphones, not even bothering to collect his change from the call. His call would send law enforcement scrambling to figure out the link between 8 random numbers and the bomb, which would give Reeves the cover he'd need to find the *real* target – an Enclave operative dialing in for orders from a handler.

Herron exited the terminal, knowing Reeves would already be searching out similar examples of eight random numbers being spoken in phone calls. The NSA would have billions of recorded calls and would also be listening in on calls being made at that very moment. There'd be a bunch of false reports, but Herron hoped at least one would have a distorted voice.

If it did, he'd have found a handler.

With luck, when he met with Reeves in 10 hours, the NSA agent would be able to put him back on the Enclave's trail. For now, though, Herron needed some sleep. In the cold night air, he joined the line of bleary-eyed travelers waiting for cabs and was inside a vehicle within a minute.

The driver was listening to the radio and news of the bomb was just breaking. He tutted. "When will they just leave us alone? We got out of Iraq years ago!"

Herron grunted a reply, closed his eyes and napped.

## 10

HERRON WATCHED the house for a few more minutes, making sure there was no movement. It was 4:00 AM, so it was unlikely he'd see any, but he hadn't survived a career as a contract killer by being stupid. He opened the door of his stolen car, climbed out and then closed it as quietly as he could. He didn't want to warn his target that doom was coming.

The bomb threat had worked a treat. The entire national security apparatus of the United States had scrambled to find it, giving Reeves all the resources he needed to finish the job. Herron had met Reeves in an alleyway and the spook had handed over what he'd found: several phone calls that featured both a distorted voice and someone reciting an eight-digit code. The most recent had originated from the house Herron was now watching.

He crossed the street, pistol in hand, and walked

around the back of the house. He wasted no time with subtlety, kicking the back door hard and sending it swinging in on its hinges to slam against the wall. He moved past it, pistol held high, walking through the laundry and into the open-plan living room that ran off it.

He cleared the house room-by-room, focusing on speed rather than stealth. He wanted to bag the handler before help could be summoned. None of the living spaces were occupied, so he moved to the bedrooms at the front of the house. He wouldn't find any children sleeping.

The first of the two bedrooms were unoccupied. That left one still to check.

He paused outside the master bedroom for only a second, took a deep breath and opened the door. With his pistol trained on the bed, he flicked on the light; the bed had been slept in, but it was currently empty.

Herron frowned. There was no ensuite bathroom or anywhere else the handler could be hiding. The whole plan with Reeves and the bomb had been geared towards this moment; could it really be a dead end?

Apart from the bed, the room had two bedside tables and a closet. Herron looked at the closet – he'd ignored it at first, but now...

He aimed low and squeezed off several shots, moving his aim along the closet. The silenced rounds tore through the timber and after three shots, a man yelled at him to stop.

Herron snarled. "You've got one chance to stay alive. Come out very slowly. You die if I see a weapon, a phone or any sort of resistance."

He took a step back as the closet door opened. A man of about 40 stepped out with his hands up. He was dressed in pajamas, unkempt and frightened, his eyes fixed on Herron's pistol. He was taken aback that such a powerful man should seem so pathetic when confronted, but it made the next steps easier. It didn't look like he'd need to spend long cracking him open to get at the secrets inside.

"Mitch, there's still time to walk away from this." The handler looked up at him for the first time, eyes pleading for mercy. "You've stayed hidden from Shade until now. This's a mistake."

*Mitch...*

Herron's eyes widened. He'd asked Reeves to help track down a handler. Was it possible they'd found *his* handler? "Are you...?"

"You got me." He shrugged. "Listen, out of respect for what our previous relationship was worth, you should disappear. You and your little band of rebels can't win. It's over."

Rage coursed through Herron. He lowered his aim and fired a shot into the man's knee. He cursed and screamed as he crumpled to the ground, but Herron ignored his cries, stepping forward and grabbing hold of the man's hair. He dragged him, kicking and yelling, out of the bedroom.

Herron hauled him downstairs and released his hair only long enough to unlock and open the front door. He stepped outside for a second and looked around. The street was empty, except for one car that was idling opposite. Herron waved at it, stepped back inside the house and dragged the handler to his feet. He howled even louder as he put weight on the knee, but Herron didn't let him fall.

"Straight to the car." Herron jammed the pistol into his side. "I don't want to hear a word out of your mouth until you're in it. Clear?"

He nodded and Herron led him all the way to the car. When he was only a few steps away, the rear door opened and Jessica smiled out at him. Herron forced the handler inside and slammed the door, knowing Jessica would keep him secure and dress the wound. He'd told her to bring a first aid kit when he called to tell her he'd tracked down a handler.

After one more good look around, Herron got into the car too. A quick drive, then it'd be time for a long chat.

* * *

The vessel rocked gently under Herron as he leaned against the rail of the boat and stared at the sea. The midday sun glistened off the water like a million diamonds, but he couldn't get out of his mind that the peace and sunshine would soon be replaced by violence and darkness – a necessary step if he was going to end the threat of the Enclave forever.

From the handler's house, Ben had driven them to the banks of the Potomac, where they'd stolen a boat and headed south into Chesapeake Bay. They were far enough from shore to do what needed doing undisturbed and the boat would also let them stay out of the Enclave's grasp while they did it.

It was time. He turned to Jessica and Ben, who were talking quietly to one another near the boat's wheel. They knew what needed to be done – what he needed to do. He was going to get answers and vengeance at the same time.

He took the steps below deck to the sleeper cabin, comprised of a double bed, a small kitchenette and an adjoining bathroom. His handler was splayed out on the bed, still out cold from the sedative Jessica had given him, so he was oblivious to the anger growing inside Herron.

Fury coursed through him as he considered all the death and destruction he'd brought under this man's orders. At the time he'd thought all his targets deserved to die, but now he had no way to be sure he hadn't been killing innocents all along.

He kicked the edge of the mattress, jolting his handler but failing to rouse him. When he failed to respond to his shouting, Herron walked back up onto the deck to grab a bucket, which he filled in the bathroom and then upended over the bed.

The handler coughed, spluttered and blinked the water from his eyes. Only then did he notice the toolbox Herron had retrieved from beside the bed. He scowled. "You're making a terrible mistake."

Herron gave a humorless laugh. "Of all the things you could say to me and with all the pain that's about to come your way, you choose the most tired movie cliché there is?"

Still sneering, he scooted up the bed to a seating position, backing away from Herron like a trapped but still dangerous animal. He was clearly used to ordering the killers around, but now Herron was calling the shots.

He dropped the toolbox onto the edge of the bed, opened it, and pulled out a box cutter. He held up the blade so the handler could see. "If you cooperate, I won't need to use this. Part of me hopes you do resist, though."

"Oh, Mitch. That little knife is the best you can do?" He shook his head. "How the hell did we get to 150 kills together?"

"149, actually." Herron pushed on the button that caused the blade to extend from the casing. "First, tell me your name."

"My name is meaningless. Taking me achieves nothing, torturing me achieves nothing, killing me achieves nothing."

"'Handler' it is, then. Now, tell me if I killed innocents. How many Enclave targets did I take down who'd done nothing wrong?"

Handler laughed. "You're a fool. Of course you killed innocents. That was the job. You got paid."

Herron clenched his teeth, resisting the urge to kill Handler right there. "There's a big meeting of all the handlers scheduled. Tell me how you all communicate with each other."

"You'll need to work for that. If I sell them out, my entire family ends up dead. But if I delay you... well, the meeting will happen and my colleagues will disperse again."

"Last chance." Herron stared at Handler for a moment, but he remained tight-lipped. "Okay."

He stepped around the bed and gave Handler the hardest backhand he could muster. He grunted when the blow landed and as he toppled sideways, Herron used his free hand to force him onto his stomach. He straddled him and pressed the blade of the knife in between Handler's shoulders, not hard enough to cut through Handler's clothing but enough so he felt it and kept still.

He used the knife to cut at Handler's clothing. It gave way to the sharp blade and within seconds he had nothing but bare, pale back to deal with. He cut into flesh, ignoring Handler's muffled screams and using his weight and strength to keep him still. He showed little care as the blade bit deep, right between his shoulder blades. The pain must've been unbearable.

Herron climbed off him. Handler writhed in pain and rolled onto his back, throwing a death stare his way. Herron laughed at the theatrics as he pocketed the knife. He'd only just started. He returned to the toolbox and dug out a heavy wrench.

"I want the location of the meeting." He slapped the wrench against his palm. "And the phone number you use to contact your colleagues."

Handler returned to a seated position and stared down at the slick of blood that had soaked the top of the bed. "Fuck yourself."

Herron smiled and stepped forward.

\* \* \*

Herron gripped the pistol in one hand and Handler's hair in the other as he led him up the stairs from below deck. He cursed and fought the whole way, but Herron was far stronger than his prisoner and not in the mood to tolerate any resistance. After a few more steps, Handler tripped and stopped climbing completely, so Herron simply dragged him by the hair.

He'd been below deck for hours. In that time, he'd beaten and tortured the hell out of Handler. He hadn't enjoyed it, but the fact he'd had him kill innocent people and then sent several killers after him and Kearns had given him the resolve he needed. Handler was bloody and broken, but he'd surrendered the answers Herron needed. Now he was worthless. A broken mess that required disposal.

When they reached the deck, Herron gave Handler's hair a final yank and sent him flying. He landed hard. Herron looked at Jessica and Ben and smiled. "I got it."

"All of it?" Jessica raised an eyebrow. "You know where the meeting is going to be? And when?"

Herron nodded. Handler, was now on all fours and looking up at him. His face was something from a horror movie. He was bruised and bloody, with one eye a dark purple and his nose clearly broken. His clothes were torn, he had cuts on his body and several broken bones. The man who'd ordered hundreds, maybe thousands, killed now looked little better than a corpse himself.

"Get it over with." Handler hissed at him.

Herron aimed the pistol and fired. "153."

Jessica looked up from the corpse. "What do you want to do about the body, Mitch?"

Herron shrugged. "We've got bigger fish to fry. Someone will find him in the next few days, but by then they'll be finished or we will be."

"Cheery." Ben said. "If I had my former handler in that position, I'd unload a magazine into him just to make sure."

Herron moved to the back of the boat. Ben had

navigated the boat to an isolated patch of coast just outside of D.C. He'd run the boat aground and killed the engines, waiting for Herron to finish his work and the time to leave the boat.

Herron climbed over the side of the boat and jumped down to the gravel and sand below. Jessica and Ben followed behind him, but he was in no mood to speak to them right now; he needed to be alone with his thoughts.

He needed to come to terms with the fact that he'd killed innocents, but he wasn't sure he ever could. Taking down Handler was the start of his redemption and destroying the Enclave would be the next step. Now he had the location of the Enclave meeting, there was a chance to smash the organization's entire leadership and fracture the network of killers into a million pieces.

If Herron had his way, he'd be the man to swing the hammer.

## 11

---

HERRON STARED down the sights of his sniper rifle. A caress of the trigger would drop another of the men who'd ordered the unjust death of so many others. This Enclave member looked entirely normal – slightly balding, dressed in an unremarkable suit, a bit overweight. Though the handlers and their master controlled some of the finest killers on Earth, it seemed they themselves were just ordinary looking people.

That suited Herron just fine. He'd had his fill of battling super-soldiers.

He lay prone on a rooftop a block away from the office building that Handler had revealed as the meeting location. By the time he Jessica and Ben had driven there from the boat, the Enclave leadership had already convened in the assigned room. There were six of them buttoned up tight on one level of the target building, sitting around a boardroom table. Nobody had entered or exited the room in some time and there was nobody else on the floor.

Herron had waited until he was confident everyone had arrived who should be attending – now the time for action was near.

He whispered. "Status check."

"*In position.*" Ben spoke first. He was on the rooftops on the other side of the target building. "*I can't see any hostiles on the ground or on the rooftops.*"

There was a slight pause, then a small crackle preceded Jessica's voice. "*I'm in position, too. No movement. Are you seeing anything, Mitch?*"

"Just a head that's ripe for a bullet." Herron grinned. "Everyone I've seen moving around the building seems calm."

"*Time to change that.*" Jessica gave a soft laugh. "*Okay, I'm about to make the call. Radio silence.*"

Herron inhaled and exhaled slowly. Jessica would be dialing the number Handler had given up under torture. It was possible he'd lied, though he'd caused so much pain he doubted it. He'd have given him anything he wanted by then. If the person on the other end answered the call, listened to the eight-digit code and then started to talk with a distorted voice, they'd know they were in the right place.

They'd have the green light to start firing.

Through his scope, Herron could see a man at the meeting table frown and look around at his five colleagues. When they stared back at him blankly, he answered the call. As he heard Jessica speak the eight-digit code that Handler had given up, the man who'd answered the call removed the phone from his ear and looked down at the phone. Then he did something very human. He looked out the window and started to talk into the phone.

"*Targets confirmed.*" Jessica's simple words sounded the death knell. "*It's them.*"

Herron grinned as his target's confused face filled his sights. "Hitting them now."

The rifle kicked hard into Herron's shoulder, the supersonic round cracking loudly as it broke the sound barrier. The result was spectacular. The window the Enclave handler had been staring out of shattered and his head exploded like it'd had an anvil dropped on it. The headless corpse dropped out of sight.

Herron worked the rifle's bolt and scanned the meeting room for more targets, even as he heard the crack of two more rifles – Jessica and Ben taking their shots. Between the three of them, they had the meeting room in a kill box, covered on three sides and every entrance covered. They'd discussed it and decided that everyone on the meeting-room floor was fair game, as was anyone on other levels who produced a weapon.

Herron inhaled and shifted his aim, drawing a bead on another target – a woman who'd drawn a pistol the moment the shooting has started. Herron exhaled as he fired, this time aiming at the center mass. The high-caliber bullet blew clean through the woman's chest. She dropped as Herron chambered another round as two more shots rang out from Jessica and Ben.

He swept back and forth for more targets, but he couldn't see any. Had they achieved utter decapitation of the Enclave? It'd almost been too easy. Though he wasn't certain everyone around the table had been a leader, any who hadn't been were still fair game. Working with scumbags had a price.

He smiled. "Clear."

"*Clear.*" Jessica spoke next.

Then there was silence.

"Ben?" Herron frowned. "Jessica, do you see him?"

"*No.*" Her voice was shaky. It was the first time since Herron had met her that her composure had slipped. "*Mitch, I—*"

He heard the boom of a rifle and Jessica grunted. Herron's eyes went wide and he ducked low – this new shooter was bound to be targeting him next. They'd gone from triumph to trepidation in less than a minute. Now he had another battle.

Survival.

"*Mitch! Mitch!*" The voice that came over the comms mocked Jessica's last cry, a voice Herron recognized only too well. "*Good job with the handlers. You beat our defenses.*"

Shade. He must've dealt with Ben, stolen his comms gear and used his rifle to take out Jessica.

Herron eased back from the rifle and crouched low. "Your leadership is eradicated, Shade. It's over."

"*Oh, you think so?*" The enemy Alpha laughed. "*None of that matters now. You're a dead man.*"

Herron snarled. With the Enclave's leaders dead, he had a choice: attack Shade head-on and probably die in the process, or return to Kearns and try to protect her, like he'd promised. His heart burned to avenge Jessica and Ben, but his head suggested the opposite.

His head won out.

There was nothing else to be achieved here. Ben and Jessica were dead and he couldn't beat Shade. He had to be content in the knowledge that the Enclave's leadership was eradicated and their atrocities would end. The mission had been a costly success, but it was time to go.

Herron drew his pistol and scanned the rooftops immediately surrounding him, but it seemed clear.

For the last time, Herron bugged out.

\* \* \*

He scrambled to the fire escape on the far side of the roof, away from where he'd been positioned. As he moved, Shade continued to curse and mock him, but he tuned it out. It was just noise. Now his decision was made, his focus screened everything else out – all that mattered was to get off the roof, steal a car, get the hell out of DC and find Kearns.

Herron ran down the fire escape to an alleyway. Cop cars flashed past, sirens blaring and lights spinning, their occupants oblivious to what had just ended on the rooftops above them. There'd now be a power vacuum amongst the most dangerous contract killers on the planet and Herron didn't plan to stick around while they fought to fill it.

There was no time for subtlety. He took two steps out of the alley and aimed his pistol at the driver of the nearest car. It took a second for the middle-aged woman at the wheel of the Ford sedan to realize what was happening, but once her mind shifted into gear she got out of the car faster than Herron would've thought possible.

"Sorry!" Herron called after her as he rounded the car and climbed inside, ignoring the cries of alarm from the woman and several bystanders.

He accelerated directly away from the buildings on which Jessica and Ben lay dead on the rooftop: Shade was still somewhere in their vicinity, so better to head in the opposite direction.

"*Mitch...*"

The female voice in his earpiece took Herron off

guard and he clenched the steering wheel so hard his knuckles went white.

Jessica?

He slammed on the brakes, turned the wheel and put his foot to the floor. The tires on the small Ford sedan squealed and other motorists rode their horns in protest as the car cut across traffic and headed back the way he'd come.

"*Wow, she's alive!*" Shade was taunting him. "*Looks like the Enclave makes us Alphas tougher than advertised. I guess it's a race to get to her now, huh Mitch?*"

Herron snarled, pulled out his earpiece and tossed it into the foot well. Now he knew Jessica was alive, he didn't want the distraction of Shade's verbal diarrhea. He zigged and zagged through traffic, driving to Jessica's building in record time. He had a lot of ground to cover, but he might just be able to beat Shade to her location – it was possible the Alpha was still on Ben's roof.

He parked on the sidewalk amid a cacophony of horns and curses, ran inside the building where Jessica had been stationed and called an elevator. He slipped inside the car, pressed for the top floor and drew his pistol as the doors closed. There was every chance Shade could've beaten him to her and he needed to be ready. The elevator came to a stop and the doors chimed open.

The hallway was deserted. Herron followed the signs to the stairs and roof access. Jessica had picked the lock to get into position a few hours earlier and the door to the stairwell opened easily. He took the stairs two at a time, until he reached another door at the top. Herron eased it open and moved onto the roof.

He spotted Jessica right away. She was slumped on her side next to her sniper rifle, blood pooled around her torso. Scanning his surroundings as he moved, he crossed to her. Her eyes were closed, so he dropped to his knees and checked for a pulse. It was there, but faint. He squeezed her wrist.

Her eyes flickered open. She looked confused at first, then relieved. "I knew you'd be back."

"Stay still." Herron kept his pistol in one hand and put pressure on the wound with the other.

She clenched her teeth in pain. "I saved your ass a bunch of times. Put me out of my misery, Mitch."

"Not going to happen." Herron shook his head. "You're not going to bleed out while I'm here to stop it. I—"

Someone moved by the stairwell. One hand still on her wound, Herron turned and aimed at the doorway. Shade's head vanished back inside as Herron fired twice – the shots pounded into the steel door.

Shade had foiled their every effort to beat the Enclave. He'd been too late to save his leaders, but even with their corpses still cooling, he kept on coming. He was everything that Herron had come to realize was wrong with the Enclave: a sadist with a God complex. With Shade alive, it wasn't enough that the Enclave's head had been cut off. The organization was still a threat.

But Jessica needed pressure on her wound to stop her bleeding out. To go after Shade now would mean leaving her...

"Mitch, he has to die." Jessica whispered, as if reading his thoughts. "There's no point saving me now. Go get him."

\* \* \*

"Be strong." Herron whispered to her and took his hand off her wound. Then he stood and advanced on Shade's position, his pistol trained on the door.

"Nice job beating me here, Mitch." Shade called out. "I didn't think you had it in you. You normally seem better at running away from danger than into it."

Herron inched closer, waiting for Shade to move. He didn't have to wait long. The barrel of a submachine gun peeked around the corner and Shade fired blind. Herron dived to the right and fired in midair as he tried to avoid the burst of fire. Both assassins missed and as Herron hit the ground Shade emerged from the doorway in search of a target.

Herron scrambled behind an air-conditioning unit as the submachine gun chattered again. He was outmatched and outgunned, Jessica was bleeding out and the only escape route was covered. He gripped his pistol tight and looked around the rooftop for options, but all he could see were more air-conditioners.

Shade was whistling tunelessly, the sound drawing closer. "We're at checkmate, Mitch. You should've tried to shoot me with your rifle. You've no chance up close."

Herron took a deep breath... then paused. A chopper was approaching, the thwack of its blades growing louder, nose pointed straight and down, the pilot punching it.

"This is the District of Columbia Metro Police!" The chopper's loudspeaker boomed as the pilot hovered over the roof. "Throw down your weapons."

There was a shooter positioned in the doorway of the helicopter. Herron swiftly recalculated: the cops were now his best chance of beating Shade and getting Jessica off the rooftop alive. He could figure the rest out later. He slowly held his pistol out and placed it on the ground, making sure to stay out of sight of Shade and his submachine gun. As soon as his pistol was down, the shooter in the doorway of the chopper shifted his attention from Herron to Shade.

Herron waited and watched, willing the cop to fire.

Shade fired first. His submachine gun barked and

sparks danced across the nose of the chopper. The windshield shattered and the pilot banked as his sniper shot back. Too slow: both the pilot and the marksman took hits.

Herron moved like a flash, snatching up his pistol and popping up from behind the air-conditioning unit. Shade was still aiming at the chopper, giving Herron a split second to act.

He unloaded the four rounds left in his magazine into Shade's center mass.

The Alpha staggered, but stayed up. He was wearing a vest. Herron cursed and ducked back under cover as Shade's return fire pounded at the steel cooling unit. Then the bolt of the submachine gun clicked forward loudly. Shade was out of ammo, too.

"Got you." Herron tossed his pistol and rounded the air-conditioner to rush at Shade. He closed the distance as fast as he could, giving his opponent no time to reload.

Shade dropped the submachine gun and held his arms wide. "I didn't think you had the guts to come at me."

Herron aimed a side kick at Shade's chest, hoping to topple his foe. Shade stepped away from the shot and used his forearms to deflect it, before lashing out with a quick jab that caught Herron in the chin, stunning him. Herron staggered back as Shade went on the attack, jabbing, striking and kicking faster than Herron thought possible. He blocked or deflected as many as he could, but his opponent was too strong. Too skilled. He took a knee to the torso and another hard shot to the head. Any attempt to fight back was quickly overwhelmed.

He was like a punch-drunk heavyweight, stumbling and exhausted. He refused to give up, but he was unable to win – the enemy Alpha was too much to deal with.

Herron gave ground, backing away from the other man's assault, inching closer to the edge of the roof. Glancing to the side, he spotted that the pilot of the police chopper had touched down on the other side of the rooftop, saving the vehicle from plummeting into the street below – Herron had been concentrating so fiercely on the fight that he hadn't noticed before. And now it was too late – the chopper was too far away. There was no other consideration, nothing that could help him, only a desperate struggle to survive.

"It was really stupid to come back here, Mitch." Shade sneered, allowing Herron to retreat a little, increasing the distance between them. "If you'd have run away, I'd have hunted you, but you might've had the chance to hide like the treacherous rat you are. Your stupidity is my gain, though. It makes it easier to take you out. The Enclave might promote me for it."

"There's nobody left to promote you, Shade.

Whatever happens to Jessica and me, the Enclave is finished."

Shade tilted his head sideways and laughed. "Do you really think that? Oh, you poor fool. Your plan almost worked. You took out all the handlers, but whoever shot at the Master didn't do very well. He's wounded, but very much alive. Paramedics are seeing to him right now. Unfortunately, you'll be too dead to finish the job."

Herron frowned. Was it possible?

Then Shade was on him again and Herron retreated under a flurry of blows, until he was less than a yard from the edge of the roof.

Any further, he'd go over the edge.

Herron took a step forward, feigned a left jab at Shade's head then tried for a right elbow strike, but his opponent was ready. Shade dealt with both blows, then delivered a shattering punch to the chin. Herron's knees went weak. It took all of his effort to avoid falling backward off the edge of the building. Instead, he fell forward and landed hard. He huddled to protect himself from kicks to his head and torso. Each time he tried to climb to his feet, he'd take another shot and collapse again.

It was over. He was spent. He couldn't beat this man.

Shade brought his foot up, poised to stamp on Herron's head.

The boot came down beside him, wide and slow.

Herron looked up.

Blood streamed from a gunshot wound in Shade's shoulder.

Jessica. It could only be her.

With a shout of fury, Herron launched himself at Shade, tackling the assassin in the midsection and lifting him off the ground. Sheer rage gave Herron the strength to ignore the blows rained down on him by the Alpha as he shoved the killer towards the edge. He stumbled to his knees only inches away, but close enough to send his nemesis over the side.

Shade screamed once... then was gone.

Herron collapsed on all fours, panting desperately to catch his breath. A little way away, Jessica was propped up with a pistol in her hand and her eyes half-closed.

He staggered over to her. "Thanks for the save."

She smiled slightly. "You looked like you needed a hand."

Herron felt for a pulse. It was weak. "We'll take the chopper out of here."

On the other side of the roof, the helicopter's rotors were still turning slowly, but the pilot had slumped forward on his stick – he'd managed to land the aircraft intact, saving the lives of those on the street below, but he hadn't survived past that. The police marksman looked dead too.

Jessica's eyes were closed now. She was almost out of time. Herron put his arms under her torso to scoop her up, but her eyes shot open and she cried out in agony. He stopped trying to lift her and the pain subsided.

"Leave me." Her voice was calm, but firm. "If Shade was right and the Master survived, you need to go after him and end this."

"No! I—" Before he'd finished speaking, her eyes turned glassy and she was gone. Herron checked for a pulse again, knowing it was futile. "Fuck!"

When his anger subsided, he prised Jessica's pistol from her hand and stood up. Though the crusade pulled him into wasn't over, her part in it was. Herron wished he could give her a fitting farewell, but there was no time. The cops would be here in minutes and he had a target to hunt.

He headed for the chopper and didn't look back.

# MORE FROM STEVE P. VINCENT

The Mitch Herron Series
*The Omega Strain*
*The Shadow Enclave*

The Jack Emery series
*Fireplay*
*The Foundation*
*State of Emergency*
*Nations Divided*
*One Minute to Midnight*

stevepvincent.com/books

# ABOUT THE AUTHOR

Steve P. Vincent is the USA Today Bestselling Author of the Jack Emery and Mitch Herron conspiracy thriller series.

Steve has a degree in political science, a thesis on global terrorism, a decade as a policy advisor and training from the FBI and Australian Army in his conspiracy kit bag.

When he's not writing, Steve enjoys whisky, sports and travel.

*You can contact Steve at all the usual places:*
stevepvincent.com
steve@stevepvincent.com

# ACKNOWLEDGMENTS

Vanessa Pratt, I'm starting to sound like a broken record, but your support is amazing.

My book fixing crew deserve ALL the beer and fried food: Dave Sinclair, Andrew McLaughlin, Gerard Burg and Janice Harris (my beta readers), Pete Kempshall (my editor), and Stuart Bache (my cover designer).

Finally, thanks to you readers. It really does mean a lot that you love my books and you let me do this for a living. I'll keep putting them out for as long as you keep caring... and probably longer!

Made in the USA
Coppell, TX
12 October 2020